I0748002

HER SISTER'S GHOST

EMMA KVĚTNA

HER SISTER'S GHOST

Copyright © 2023 by Emma Května

For more information visit: www.emmakvetna.com

Cover & Interior Design by Emma Května
Cover Artwork by Toon Joosen
Copyediting by Chelsea Comeau

ISBN: 978-1-7390608-0-0

First Edition: July 2023

HER SISTER'S GHOST

For sisters everywhere

EMMA KVĚTNA

Reaching for the hot chai latte from the barista's outstretched hand struck Genevieve with the memory of when her sister made them a pot of tea once, brewed so carefully, set out so daintily in cups and saucers like they were royalty, only to discover that the sugar Claire had stirred into their drinks was actually salt, causing them to throw out the first-poured cups – which were always the best tasting – and settle for the second cup.

Genevieve wasn't sure why cinnamon chai latte reminded her of that; perhaps because it wasn't too long ago that she used to order tea, milk and sugar, the drink of choice she and her sister had shared since childhood. But now she'd become a cliché. Your basic millennial sipping a smooth chai latte during autumn. At least she wasn't wearing Uggs (yet).

Why did certain things have to be a cliché anyway? Was it also a cliché that her sister no longer spoke to her or anyone in their family anymore? Or was that simply just a common tragedy? A "that's life" moment. Genevieve had seen other broken families growing up, but did not think it could happen to her own.

Nowadays, she saw it at work as well. Single parents – usually the woman – dropping their toddlers off for daycare. Young couples coming to pick up their kids and barely speaking to each other. Kids whose parents were totally absent, and it was the aunt, uncle or grandparent picking them up.

Genevieve leant on the café door and stepped outside, wondering who invented the word "normalcy." What was *normal*? Perhaps what that person had meant to say was "natural." It's natural to have a family that stays together, but it's not normal.

The first sip of the frothy cinnamon topping was delicious. Genevieve wondered if Claire drank tea lattes now, too, or if she'd converted to coffee like so many people did. Genevieve tried to believe she really didn't care, but she did. It was a simple thing one ought to know about one's sister. She felt it was sad that she didn't know, like it was yet another dead part of her sister that she kept finding. A memory of some truth, but one that may very well have changed. That's what five years apart did – erased things, skewed things, separated things. People grew and evolved, there was no doubt about that. Genevieve was so far removed from the version of herself that Claire had blocked on Facebook.

She wanted Claire to see her now and make an updated, informed decision about whether or not to still shun her.

The air was crisp, and the leaves crunched beneath Genevieve's boots. Work was done for the day, the kids safely back in their broken homes. Genevieve knew she was avoiding the thought that'd been brewing at the back of her skull since she'd learnt two weeks ago that her sister would be in town that weekend. She could do it. She could go see her. But should she? Genevieve didn't even know what she'd say if she saw Claire again. But at the same time, she had lots to say. When she was feeling nostalgic and weepy, which happened a few times a year, she'd run through all the options in her head and have an imaginary conversation with her sister, predicting what the responses might be.

–Hi, how are you?

–I don't want to talk.

–Hi, how's things?

–Why are you here? I thought I was dead to you.

–Hi Claire, remember me?

–No.

In all instances, nothing Genevieve said mattered.

But in three days, her sister would be in town again. That was a fact. Genevieve had been remembering her a lot lately. One of the kids at the daycare reminded her exactly of Claire when she was four years old. Jaw-length, dark brown hair, round face, small mouth. Always quiet and unassuming but secretly hilarious.

At that age during bath time one night, Genevieve remembered when they were both sitting in the tub playing with the shampoo and conditioner bottles. Genevieve lifted the shampoo over Claire's head and squeezed. The transparent yellow goo dripped down the front of Claire's head, missing most of her hair and threatening to slide down her face. Claire dipped her chin so the shampoo wouldn't get into her eyes. Then she threatened to cry by opening her mouth, her hands becoming fists. Genevieve, always quick to do anything to stop her little sister from crying, squeezed shampoo down the front of her own head and said, "Look, see?" Claire gave her sister such a confused side-eye that Genevieve couldn't help but laugh. Then Claire laughed, too.

Genevieve hadn't heard her sister's laugh in over five years. And she didn't know for sure anymore what Claire took in her tea.

In three days, though, she could find out. She could offer to take her out to tea. She didn't think anything bad could really come of that.

–Hey, I heard you were here. I know it's been a

while. Can we just get some tea?

–I don't think that's a good idea.

–Hey, I knew you'd be here and I know you hate me, but can we just talk over a tea?

–I suppose that'd be fine.

It was decided then.

Genevieve drank the last of her latte and lodged it into a garbage can. She rode the subway for two stops and then crossed the street at the lights, walked another block to her apartment building and let herself in. She bounded up the flight of stairs feeling good about her decision, but already there was a metallic knot in her gut. Apprehension. Potential. The unknown.

She unlocked her apartment door, threw the keys on the table and hung up her coat and bag. In the living room, floating at the window, caught in the light in such a way that Genevieve almost didn't see her, was an unmistakable form. A white, transparent spectre of something that looked just like Claire.

* * *

I don't know what came before, but all I see right now is the city stretched out one way and tall buildings blocking my view the other. And people down below, marching along the sidewalks, some obediently waiting at the lights for the little green man to tell them to walk. All of them know where they've come from and where they're going. It's more than I can say for myself; I'm simply here. In this room. I know it's Genevieve's apartment, but I don't know how I know that.

I hear the key in the lock and turn around. Watch as my sister enters, removes her coat. Bag. Looks up, startled.

At first, my sister says nothing. She's frozen across the room, and I know she's trying to figure things out. But she'll never get there. She frowns, blinks. Frowns. Finally, she lets out a breath.

"Is this why I've been thinking about you lately?" she says. "Because you're dead?" Her eyes water. "When did this happen?"

"Who says I'm dead?" I ask.

Genevieve gestures to me. "Have you seen you? There's barely anything to see." She collapses onto the couch, wipes her nose. "Why are you here if you're not dead?"

I shrug. "I don't know. Why not?"

"You never made any sense." Genevieve sighs.

"Maybe you just never listened."

Genevieve's not listening now. She stares right

through me.

"I can't believe you're dead."

I twist my mouth to the side and drift to the middle of the room. "I don't think I am. I can still feel I'm alive."

"Mom and Dad are gonna be so devastated," Genevieve says before her face falls into her palm. "You don't talk to them for five years, and now this."

"*You're not listening,*" I say again. "I'm alive. I know I am, really."

Genevieve grabs a tissue from the mostly empty tissue box on her coffee table. She blows her nose. "That really doesn't seem right."

I roll my eyes. "I think I'd know if I were dead."

"That makes no sense coming from you in your current state."

"Why don't you ever believe me?" I spin around to face the mirror on Gen's wall, but of course I don't see myself in it. Only Gen, looking at empty space. Then I remember something she said. "What did you mean about the five-year thing?"

* * *

Of all the reunion scenarios Genevieve had played out in her head, she'd never imagined one like this. There she was. Claire. Or, at least, the ghost version of Claire, and this ghost didn't have a clue in the world that it had been five years since she'd talked to Genevieve. And that that had been a choice she, living Claire, had made.

Genevieve would have liked to say that's classic Claire, always forgetful. But it wasn't. Claire had the memory of an elephant. She remembered every single little thing forever, and it had driven Genevieve nuts growing up. Claire liked to live in the past. Genevieve liked to enjoy the present and sometimes fret about the future. She remembered when she found ripped-up paper in her bedsheets one evening, stuffed under the covers. The paper was a handwritten chatlog of sorts, before they had access to cellphones, a series of secret notes written between Claire and Genevieve the week before. One girl would write a message to the other and slip it under her bedroom door, then the other would write back on it and slip it under the other one's door, and so on and so forth. That particular written conversation was about making arrangements to play a game of make-believe – Genevieve couldn't remember what about what exactly – but Claire became upset when Genevieve reneged on her promise to play, and instead went off to visit a friend in town on her bike. A week later, and Claire was still mad, while Genevieve had forgotten all about it. She immediately showed their mother the shredded note in her bed that evening. Claire got told off. They didn't play make-believe much after that, all because of Claire's begrudging memory.

Genevieve scrutinized the ghost before her. It was definitely Claire – long, billowing brown hair, an oval face that met in a delicate, pointed chin, eyes that half-mooned when she smiled. She took after their mother's English roots, while Genevieve was taller, with shoulder-length ash-blonde hair, high cheekbones, larger nose, and a strong chin. That was more their father's Scandinavian side. But both girls shared the same eye shape and colour: hazel irises, short lashes, and slightly arched brows. People always said they couldn't possibly be related – if it weren't for the eyes. But whenever they were placed next to their older brother, people often asked if Claire was adopted; Peter shared far more features with Genevieve than Claire.

The ghost version of Claire was partially transparent, some sort of shade between white and grey. Strangely, she wore an outfit Genevieve hadn't seen since their teenage years: boyfriend jeans with paint stains, converse sneakers, and a tucked-in black tank top underneath an oversized, unbuttoned plaid shirt, sleeves rolled up. It was Claire's go-to outfit for painting in her studio. The plaid shirt in real life was coloured with reds and blacks, and the boyfriend jeans were a light-wash denim. Claire had worn the outfit a lot in their teens because she liked to be comfy and didn't care for fashion. Genevieve on the other hand had grown to appreciate putting together a great outfit and always told Claire how juvenile the painting outfit made her look whenever she wore it.

It must have been the outfit Claire was wearing when she died. Genevieve couldn't believe she still had it. That seemed embarrassing, so she didn't bring it up. She continued scrutinizing ghost Claire. She was looking for a sign of how she died, like an injury of some sort. Any clue that could tell them what happened to her. Not that it mattered anymore. But it'd be nice to know so that she could tell their parents.

Oh God – their parents. She knew how they'd react. Dad would feel guilty that he'd acted so indifferent towards the end about Claire disowning them (it wasn't that he was okay with it; he was just too angry to fret over it any longer), and Mom, well – she may just die herself. Every month or two for the past five years, she'd sent Claire an email to update her and ask how she was, and to apologize for anything that she'd done wrong. The emails, of course, never arrived, because Claire had blocked them. Genevieve didn't see what the point in this ritual was, but her mother seemed to think that one day, if Claire ever unblocked her, Claire would suddenly receive a slew of emails from her mother that were waiting to be delivered, and then Claire would see how much she was always loved. Genevieve had tried to explain to her mother countless times that that was not how unblocking someone's email worked.

Her mother had also continued to search for Claire online, but she was blocked from all of Claire's social media accounts. Even Claire's boyfriend, Ryan, had blocked her. But he hadn't blocked Genevieve yet, or at least he'd forgotten to. Which was how Genevieve had found out that Ryan and Claire would be visiting town for the annual Art & Print Fair. It was something Claire and Genevieve used to go to all the time, but they stopped when they both entered college. The fact that Ryan had posted online that they were going to the show made Genevieve wonder if that meant they had moved back to the area at some point without telling Claire's family, or if they were just flying in specifically for the fair itself. If the latter, it seemed a pricey thing to do just to go to a weekend fair. Genevieve wondered what sort of money they made now. What jobs did they have? They had both started with art in college – that's how they met – but were they now doing art-related jobs? Or had Claire given that up as well? Genevieve would have liked to ask ghost Claire for the answers, but she had a feeling ghost Claire wouldn't know about any of that either.

Since Genevieve's discovery of Ryan's post, she had no intention of telling her parents about the fact that Claire would be at the fair until after she'd had a chance to meet with Claire herself. Genevieve feared that one or both of her parents would rush over and unintentionally scare Claire away. Their parents still lived in the area where the girls had grown up, which was a seven-hour drive away from Genevieve's current apartment. She liked to be close to her parents without having to take a flight and enjoyed going home on weekends when she felt she might burst in the city, but Claire had gone to school in a whole different province at the other end of the country. She'd made new friends and had rarely come home except at holidays, and it had all been okay for a while. The sisters FaceTimed regularly. Claire would FaceTime their parents monthly. All was well, until it wasn't.

* * *

I've seen that look before, that one of incredulity on Genevieve's face every time she thought I said something stupid when we were kids.

"What do you mean, 'What do I mean'?" she asks.

"You said I haven't talked to Mom and Dad in five years. That doesn't sound like me."

Genevieve took a deep breath and exhaled shakily. "It wasn't just them you didn't talk to. It was me as well. And Peter. And Grandma. And Uncle Jeff." She begins listing off names on her fingers. "Aunt Maggie, Henry, Brandon. You even blocked your art teacher from high school."

"Ms. Callahan?" I reply. "Her classes *made* me."

"I know. Your first art show." Genevieve is silent, studying me. Her eyes are dry now but red rimmed. "You really don't know?"

I shrug. The only emotion I feel is low-key bliss, so I really can't relate to why I would do such a thing. I've never felt this way before. I feel generally good. And I'm not even sad or angry that I'm a ghost. Except I do know, somehow, that I haven't died. That is yet to come.

"So what *do* you remember?" Genevieve asks.

I remember her. I remember the house we grew up in: an Arts and Craft home with a wraparound porch, a spooky, undone basement and circular windows nestled in the dormers. I remember the two dogs we had, Jezebel and Sparky. Jez and Spark. I remember walking next to Gen every day to our elementary school and then taking separate buses to different high schools because I wanted to go to the one that had a special arts program, but Genevieve didn't want to go because it was a Catholic school, and she always claimed to be atheist.

"Everything," I reply. "I remember everything." I float back over to the window and watch all the live bodies again walking around. They aren't small because we aren't that high up. "I remember where we lived and grew up. I remember when Jezebel had to be put down when I was 14 and you were 16. I had never seen you cry so hard. You barely ate for weeks and never left Sparky's side."

Genevieve shifts in her seat on the couch. I can tell she's reached for another tissue.

"We never got to tell you when Sparky died."

I turn around.

"He had tumours all over his body. We put him down four years ago," she says, "but we had no way of telling you because you blocked all our calls and messages."

Poor Sparky. An image flashes through my mind of a long-haired black dog running towards me, nothing but glee in his face. I find this all very hard to believe, the fact that I would have blocked my family, but I'm not cross. I'm so at peace being here. There's just that bliss feeling enveloping me. But that's not even the right word for it. It's something else. And it's everywhere. I feel this must be a ghost thing, this feeling. Did I feel this way when I was alive? I can't remember. I only remember Gen, and being in her shadow for many years. Sometimes I was fine with it, sometimes not. I remember all my years at high school, and I remember graduating. But then it gets blurry after that. Things get blurry.

I choose my next words carefully. "Why would I do that?" I float over to the couch and sit next to Gen. "Why would I shut my own family out?"

Genevieve shakes her head, pauses, seems to choose *her* next words carefully. "It's not exactly something I can just summarize in a few sentences. I don't even fully understand it myself."

"Well, at this point, I know even less than you do," I say. "So just try." In my heart, though, if I even have one, I feel none of this really matters. I don't feel like anything can affect me, because I'm no longer human. But I keep this to myself. "Tell me what happened."

* * *

It was eerie to be this close to her sister again, staring through her rather than at her. Genevieve had so many questions – how did she die? Did it hurt? *When* did she die? It must have just happened. Maybe Mom and Dad were getting the call at that moment from the police that Claire Fowler's body had been found at the scene of an accident. Maybe they'd be calling Genevieve any second to tell her the bad news. Ghost Claire seemed to think she was still alive somewhere – that's what she kept saying, at least. But she was clearly wrong. Growing up, Genevieve always felt that her little sister generally didn't know what she was talking about, and it seemed she was the same in death, too. Or maybe she was in denial. Either way, Claire clearly did not have a good grasp on the reality of the situation.

Genevieve was disappointed that the Claire sitting before her had no clue about her own self-inflicted exile from their family, and yet Genevieve was surprised to feel that she was also kind of relieved about this. Because now that Claire was here, Genevieve really had no words to begin addressing that whole thing. She needed to ease into it. If ghost Claire *had* been up to speed, Genevieve would've had to begin there right away. It would have been the elephant in the room. But it wasn't. And it was up to Genevieve to bring it up at her own pace. The upper hand, just like she liked.

But where to begin. The distance? The boy? The journal? The fateful art show? The emails? The indifference of it all?

—It's simpler if I just show you.

Genevieve got up and grabbed her phone. In the Facebook Messenger app, she found the message thread between herself and Claire. It was way down at the bottom, of course. Genevieve hadn't looked at the thread of messages in at least three years. She couldn't quite bring herself to delete them, and over time they became buried beneath all the other message threads from other people. People she'd met at school, at work, or through other friends. Some of them were people that she was now closer with than she'd ever been with Claire.

Genevieve kept scrolling until she recognized the profile photo of a blank facial silhouette. The name simply said *Facebook User*. Genevieve opened the thread and scrolled up past the last messages she'd sent the day Claire blocked her. It was their last fight. Why couldn't Claire just come home for Thanksgiving, Genevieve wanted to know. Claire said Genevieve would never understand. Genevieve told her to get over things and stop being so melodramatic. *Stop being so childish.* That had sent Claire over the edge, and after exchanging some heated words, Genevieve suddenly couldn't send messages anymore or see Claire's profile. She immediately tried phoning her sister, but it went straight to voicemail. She left a few messages but realized Claire wasn't getting those either.

Genevieve scrolled up to November 2017 and found the message that Claire had sent, the message that, in Genevieve's mind, was the beginning of things.

OMG!! I've met a guy. We have to facetime. Hurry uuuup!

Ryan was his name. Also in Fine Arts. Printmaking. Digital drawing background, originally, but he claimed it "wasn't real enough." He wanted to be doing something with his hands more, a real craft that he could learn. Something with a history he could study the original techniques and methods of. No more backlit screens, he'd said. Genevieve thought this came across as a bit pompous, but she tried not to judge too harshly until she met him in person. Apparently, he'd been into printmaking in his teens, but was told there's no money in it, and wouldn't it be better to build on his drawing skills and get into digital art? That way, he could at least make money as a graphic designer for business people when he wasn't collaborating with other artists. Genevieve had always gotten the feeling that Ryan's parents wanted him to do graphic art as a backup plan, a practical skillset more in demand. But he was an only child with artistic whims, so they ultimately let him decide.

–This was the day you met Ryan Matar. He was your first boyfriend.

And the only one, too. Because they were sisters, Genevieve of course knew every crush Claire had ever had, and she also knew that none of them had gone anywhere. And because Genevieve was able to see Ryan's Twitter account, she knew that Claire was still with Ryan even to this day. Or, at least, she was until she died.

Genevieve wondered what sensitive-artist Ryan was doing right now, if he was grieving uncontrollably, likely at his parent's place, with an icepack on his porcelain forehead. Speaking of parents, why hadn't either of her own called with the news yet? It was almost like even the authorities knew that the Fowlers were cut off from their daughter and were ok with upholding this status quo.

–I'd never seen you so happy about someone before.

Genevieve scrolled through, reading out some of the messages that Claire had sent her about Ryan throughout the month of November and into December. During that time, Ryan rather quickly told Claire he loved her and proposed that she meet his parents over Christmas, but Claire already had plans to fly home that December, which she did. Genevieve and Peter came home too.

She remembered during Christmas Eve dinner, Claire left the table to answer a call from Ryan and didn't come back. Genevieve found her later on up in her room, sitting on the bed giggling while talking to Ryan on FaceTime.

The whole holiday, Claire was distracted. When they went on their annual sister walk in the snow through the neighbour's fields with Sparky, all Claire did was either not speak at all or talk about Ryan. Genevieve asked her how her painting was going. Claire shrugged; she hadn't painted in weeks.

Claire was an excellent expressionist painter. She was serious about her craft and saved up to buy a premium oil paint set when she was just 12. There was one painting in particular that Genevieve had always loved. The colours were dark and moody, and the scene depicted some sort of figure being washed away in a raging river – or perhaps the figure was driving the river to rage. Claire painted it when she was 18 and still living at home during her last two years of high school. The painting made Genevieve feel mysterious and otherworldly. Claire, however, had always said she hated it.

Ryan was so inspired by Claire's skills as an artist, a "true artist" he'd said, that it inspired him to get back into printmaking. *But he lacks confidence because of his parents' doubts. I can help him through that, though,* Claire had told Genevieve on their walk through the glistening pine trees, the sound of Sparky's dog tags tinkling in the dry air.

* * *

Genevieve tells me about this Ryan fellow, but I feel nothing. I watch her lips move as she talks, the bottom slightly plumper than the top. The left corner always drawn slightly more down than the right. I can't summon a face or a voice of the boy she's speaking of, can't remember any time spent with him. It must have happened after the blurred parts. It doesn't matter, though. None of this matters. Just that feeling of *bliss.* I let her talk.

"It was a weird Christmas. Our last Christmas with all of us together. Everyone noticed how different you were. Even Peter. He thought you were just being a typical girl, giddy about some guy. I'm sure he thought the whole thing was silly, but he didn't really say much about it. I could see you were changing, though. Or maybe you were just being more of your true self.

It was your third year of college. Over the Christmas break, you told me things on our walks and car rides into town, but I could tell it wasn't the whole story. Things about Ryan, things about your new art friends. At the time I didn't realize it, but that's when you started slipping away. Mom asked if we wanted to go to Beechum's Farm to get our tree, just like we always did. I said yes, of course, but you said no. You stayed home and probably spent the whole time on the phone to Ryan. Mom asked me in the car if there was something going on with you. I felt in that moment I should have had an answer. *The* answer. I was your sister after all, and Mom was asking me because it was a given that, of all people, *I* should know what was going on with you, right? But I didn't have a good answer for her. I just said you were distracted."

Genevieve pauses, the phone still held in her hand. I've been listening to her, but I'm caught between feeling everything is all right and everything will be okay. It occurs to me that maybe ghosts aren't capable of feeling negative things. I don't think I could be sad right now even if I tried. I'm still not sure why I'm here or how I arrived, but it's nice to be here.

"Where was Dad in all this?" I ask.

Genevieve frowns. "You don't remember? They got divorced when you were finishing high school."

That doesn't register for me either. When I think of Dad, I am struck by a memory of him helping me ride a bike that had a maroon frame and white tassels on the handle bars. I picked up biking faster than Genevieve, and he was so impressed by that. Genevieve was grumpy about it, of course. Once I figured out how to bike on my own, I rode circles around her with Peter, following him over a small jump he'd set up with a broken board. He was the cool older brother who I didn't have really anything in common with, but for whom I would probably do anything to impress.

"They divorced when I was 18?"

Genevieve nods.

I turn on the sofa so that I'm sitting straight ahead. "Hmm. That's when my memory gets blurry."

Genevieve twists now so that she's facing me. "Why didn't you tell me that before?"

I shrug. "I dunno."

"That must be important for some reason."

She goes to give my shoulder a light shove, as if to say, *Come on now, you should have known that.* I'm very familiar with the gesture. But her hand goes right through me. We both look down at my shoulder, then

25

back at each other.

"Okay, you know what's really weird about all this?" Genevieve asks.

Before I can reply, her phone rings. She jumps, then her face blanches when she sees the screen.

"Oh my God," she says. "This is it."

I look down at the caller ID. It's our mother.

Gen gets up and answers the phone. "Hi, Mom." She paces around the room, and I ponder how I feel about our mom. She loves art like I do. I think it's because of her that I became an artist. She constantly took me to art galleries and art shows down in the city when I was growing up. These were our special trips, just me and her. Genevieve was never interested in going. Peter had other things to do. Dad was always working. It was better that it was just us anyway because Mom and Dad fought so much. I always figured that's just how parents were: angry. It felt a little like maybe that was our fault as kids, and I could never understand why Gen or Peter didn't get that. Mom was hard to talk to because of her issues with Dad, so any chance we got to go to the gallery I relished, because it was a rare moment that she was happy and at peace.

Gen catches my eye and I whisper, "Tell Mom I said hi."

She scowls at me and says, "Shh! What? Oh, nothing Mom, just the neighbours."

A moment later, she hangs up the call and sits back down on the couch.

"Well, *that* was actually the weirdest part."

She pauses for effect and I say, "What happened?" She was always pausing for effect, and I remember how much it used to annoy me as a kid.

"Mom called but she didn't mention anything about you being dead. She was totally normal. She just asked if I could pick up something for her before I come home next weekend."

"What's odd about that?"

"I assumed if you had died, the police would have notified Mom and Dad by now. So I thought that was her calling to tell *me* the news. But it wasn't."

See, all is well. Everything will be fine.

Genevieve locks eyes with me. "I guess you were right."

* * *

Okay, so maybe the real Claire *was* still alive somewhere. That was good. Genevieve would be able to see for herself in three days, but for now she felt less panicked about the vitality of her sister.

The question still remained, though, a question in the shape of Claire's ghost. She had to help Claire remember. Was that the key to helping her pass on, even though she wasn't really dead, apparently?

Genevieve shook her head. It was all too much. She needed a drink. Genevieve went to the kitchen and pulled out an opened bottle of red wine from the fridge. She jokingly asked Claire if she could pour her a glass too. Ghost Claire sent her a deadpan look.

Genevieve took a big swig and then poured some more. When was the last time she'd had a glass of wine with the real Claire? Had they ever? By the time Genevieve was in her third year at college, Claire was nearly 19 and starting first year at a college that was a five-hour flight away. She would have drunk more with her girlfriends in first year than she ever would with Genevieve, before or after that.

Getting drunk with her sister...yet another missing milestone.

Genevieve took another sip. Mom had sounded like her typical self on the phone. Controlled voice but with a slight edge of panic to it for no good reason. She wanted Genevieve to pick up particular a floor lamp in town, for the living room at home. Genevieve was glad her mother had decided to keep their childhood home. It was Dad who had eventually moved out into a bungalow one town over. It broke his heart to leave, and for quite a while, he moped around in his new place. Being divorced at aged 56 wasn't supposed to be in the cards for him, plus he was also unhappy that Claire had decided to move so far away for school at the time. *If that's where she wants to go, though, then that's fine with me.* But things with him were never really just fine.

The sun outside was starting to set, casting Genevieve's side of the building into shadow. She drew the curtains and took her wine back to the couch. She took a long sip and then stared at her sister, who had gotten up to study the bookcase.

For a moment, Genevieve thought it was really her, the real Claire, and her heart swelled. She was here. The essence of her was really here, but she also wasn't. The way ghost Claire was bending down to read the spines of the books made it seem like she was someone Genevieve had just met. A new friend stopping by for the first time, showing interest in everyday things. Genevieve figured that's how it actually would be, if real Claire were to show up at her apartment. Genevieve would invite her in, unintentionally act awkward after all the missing time between them, and make innocuous small talk. Claire would feel the need to instinctively head for the bookcase, a safe area, something to talk about. She would use the books as a distraction, seeing for the first time, in many cases, the kinds of books Genevieve was now reading.

They had both been readers growing up and used to share books, but it was Genevieve who had taken a prolonged interest in reading into adulthood. With five years passed between them, her tastes had changed as she'd evolved.

She could imagine the way Claire's long brown hair would cascade as she leant down, tilting each book out of its place so she could see the cover and decide if it interested her or not. She was always drawn to visuals first, wanting to see how things presented themselves. Genevieve, however, mostly ignored the covers and always read the backs first. She would be so excited to tell her sister about the books she'd been collecting. It would be a welcomed relief. A sign that maybe things would be okay.

But as she watched ghost Claire eyeing the books, unable to physically pick up any of them, all Genevieve felt was empty.

* * *

"Do you live here with anyone?" I straighten and turn to look at my sister, waiting for her answer.

"No. Just me."

"Any boyfriends?" I ask with an eyebrow wiggle.

Genevieve snorts, but with a smirk. "More like a friend-with-benefits situation." She sips her wine. "But mainly I've been busy with work, and I'm just living my best, mostly single life right now. Don't even have a cat."

"Why not? I thought you loved animals."

Genevieve looks offended. "I do still. But I go out a lot to events and things. I want to travel more too, so I'm just not ready to get a pet again." She pauses as I float over to some pictures on the wall. "Hey, do you remember that trip we always said we wanted to do together?"

Something twigs in my thoughts. Hmm. A trip. Just me and Genevieve. "Was it somewhere with a beach?"

"Yes. We always said we wanted to go to Bali. It was right after we saw the movie *Eat Pray Love,* remember?"

I smile. "Yeah, I remember."

I mean, I don't remember watching the movie, but I remember Genevieve's face afterwards. She was so animated and said that we could ride horses down the beach and live in a villa. She wasn't interested in the idea of meeting a man there like in the movie; she just loved the location and wanted it to be our adult sisterly adventure. She said we could get mopeds and explore the villages, maybe even rent a boat if we were rich enough. I thought it was a grand idea. We made a vow to go together once we were both graduated from college.

"This is going to sound silly, but...I've actually been saving up for that trip," Genevieve says. "In fact, I have enough to go, but I haven't yet."

"Because of me?"

She nods. "I've been waiting, thinking that when all of this gets resolved, if it does, we can go to Bali like we always said we would. Make up for lost time."

I wish I could say something comforting, but it's not my place. It's odd that although I'm the person she's referring to, I'm also not. All I can think is that I would love to go, we *should* go. We should go right now. But it's not the same.

"Anyway," she says. "It's a silly fantasy now."

I shrug. "It's not silly. And it wasn't always a fantasy." She doesn't say anything else, so I ask, "What do you do for work?"

"I work at a daycare," she replies. When she sees the confused expression on my face she adds, "It's not what you think. I help with their marketing and some admin stuff mostly."

"I was gonna say," I give a little laugh. "You hate kids!"

She smiles and shakes her head. "I never hated them. I just didn't want them. Still don't, but I do like them. They have a good energy. They're so easy to entertain."

I like how musical my laugh sounds, and I drift behind the couch, come around to face Gen. "I remember when Uncle Ben and Auntie Gail visited, and we looked after our baby cousin. She was so cute. I was always good with kids, but you were so stoic around them. I'm shocked you work in a daycare now."

"Yeah, well, a lot's changed," she says, picking up her wine glass again. "You know, this version of you would have been a great mother. You seem so happy and...light."

It's true, I do feel light, and not just because I'm a ghost. "I know. Ever since I got here, I've just had this feeling of pure harmony constantly humming around me. I just know there's nothing bad where I'm from." I give a sigh and settle into the armchair. "Why do you think I would make a better mother than the real Claire? Is she that miserable?"

Genevieve tucks her legs up under herself on the couch and sips more wine. "Honestly, I don't know what she's like now. I have no idea. I assume she is happy with her little life, with Ryan and…whatever her job is now. And I don't know that she *wouldn't* make a good mother. It's more so that I simply don't know, one way or the other. God, maybe she even already has a child. Who knows? I really couldn't say. She's a real stranger to me now." Gen flips her hair over to one side. The words are spilling out of her just like the wine is spilling down her throat. She sets the empty glass on the coffee table. "She – you – will be here in three days, and I decided today that I want to see her. I feel it's time and that it's something I must do. And why not, right? She's *my* sister and I'll see her if I want to. Maybe that's why you're here. To prep me. Or stop me. Good luck there." She giggles. "Who the hell knows? I sure don't."

She really cares, doesn't she. I know she thinks she's babbling because she's feeling drunk, but she's a big feeler and always has been. Things are coming back to me now. There used to be a toy that she loved and carried with her everywhere. Some sort of bear or horse. Peter took it and taunted her with it. She cried and cried, even when he gave it back to her. He asked her why she was still crying, and she said because the bear (or horse) was still scared, and it didn't know why it had to go through that. And she was sad because she would never be able to make it understand, since it was just a toy that couldn't speak. Peter told her to stop being such a cry-baby. Then I tried to give her my own toy, and she told me to go away.

The tragedy growing up was how much Gen had to suppress that side of her because of our parents. There was only enough room in the house for one focus of emotional drama, and our parents combined took the cake. Married too young, happy at first with Peter, and then steadily becoming unhappier with each subsequent child. I remember lots of fights about money. Lots of tears.

I remember Dad buying Mom a ring once. I must have been around six. I snuck downstairs and watched him give her this jewelled ring, and she just wept. *Why did you waste money on that?* I knew it was better to be out of sight when Mom cried, so I went back upstairs to the room I shared with Gen. She was sleeping in her bed. I wanted to wake her up but decided to climb back into my own and lie awake, listening to Mom and Dad's murmurs downstairs.

I turn my attention back to Gen. "So what did I do next then," I ask, "after Christmas?"

Genevieve's eyelids droop, and she leans back on the couch. "You went back to school for second semester, and that's when things got weirder. You wanted our parents to meet Ryan on FaceTime, so they did, individually. I was there visiting Dad when he talked to Ryan for the first time, so that's when I got to meet Ryan as well. He wasn't what I expected. You had made him sound like he was this mature, super smart, worldly guy. But he was just a kid."

"What did he look like?"

Gen smirks. "Guess he wasn't that great if you can't remember him." I can tell she's pleased about that, so I let her have it. "Well, he had this mop of curly blond hair, skin somewhere between olive toned and pale, angular jaw, dimple in one cheek. He was attempting to grow a moustache, but the hair was very fine above his lip. He had blue eyes that were kind of puppy dog like, like Paul McCartney's."

"Who's that?"

Genevieve brings her palm to her face. "You don't remember who Paul McCartney is?"

"Nope." I only feel that Gen is important in my world.

Gen sighs and carries on. "Well, anyway, that's what he looked like. He was a bit taller than you, with an average build. I guess all in all I could see why you were attracted to him, but he was kind of out of line that day."

"How so?"

"On the call, he was very formal with Dad, calling him 'Sir' and all, which was fine. I think most guys do that with their girlfriends' parents. But then they both started low-key arguing about politics. Ryan's thinking was a bit naïve. He was only 21 after all. And Dad was politely trying to explain to him why he wasn't seeing the whole picture. Anyway, about an hour after the call ended, Claire phoned Dad and said he had offended Ryan." Gen gave a laugh. "Dad was speechless. He didn't really know what to say to that. Claire wanted him to apologize, apparently. Dad was stunned but agreed, and before he knew what was happening, Ryan got on the phone. Dad quickly said some sort of half-ass apology, then hung up and said to me, 'What the hell was all that about?' That was his first impression of Ryan, and it hasn't changed since. In fact, it's gotten worse."

I remember having crushes growing up and always being so eager to gossip with Gen about what some guy had said to me at school or what glance he'd thrown my way. But I don't remember being so boy-crazy that I would end up doing that to my dad. "I wonder why that was important to me, the apology."

"Oh," Gen says, "it gets better."

* * *

Ryan had not made a good impression on their mother either, the first time they'd talked. Finally, it was something their parents could unite over – their dislike of Ryan Matar.

–A very off-putting boy.

–Who does he think he is?

They were not particularly good at hiding their feelings towards him. They refused to pander to Claire's whims about what they should or shouldn't say around Ryan, or how they should or shouldn't act.

Genevieve remembered the night she got a call from her sister. She was out with a guy (the date was going so-so), and though her phone was on silent, she happened to glance at it right when Claire was calling. Some sort of sister telepathy. Grateful for an excuse to leave her date, she said she had to take the call and went outside the restaurant.

Claire almost never called her out of the blue like that. They weren't really the calling type. They used to text frequently, and message on Facebook, and they FaceTimed when they had more to say than it took to type out, which was often. A random phone call though, was a sign of an emergency.

–You were distraught on the phone. I hadn't heard you cry like that in a long time.

Even still, Genevieve could remember the sound of her sister's sobs. She thought she'd been in an accident and was calling her first because she was scared to call Mom or Dad. That felt like a good reason to call your sister unexpectedly. *I've crashed the car* or *I dropped Grandma's ring down the sink.* But it wasn't that. It was Ryan. He'd told Claire how inadequate her parents always made him feel. And he said he couldn't date someone who had such horrible parents. So, he'd broken up with her.

Growing up, Claire had largely kept her feelings to herself, always writing in her diary, so Genevieve was surprised Claire would even bring this issue to her. Why not one of her girlfriends from art class? But no, here she was on the phone, pouring her heart out to her sister about this guy. Why didn't Mom and Dad like him, she wanted to know. *I just want them to like him.* Genevieve began to feel bad for making fun of Ryan so much behind his back. Maybe he wasn't all that bad, and Claire was truly in love. So what if he liked printmaking? So what if he was naïve about certain things? Weren't they all at some point or another? For a moment, she was mad that she'd allowed herself to be so swayed by their parents' perception of Ryan. She should have listened to Claire more. She felt special that Claire chose to call her in that moment. But she also hadn't forgotten Ryan had made Claire cry by giving her this alarming ultimatum.

Genevieve listened until Claire had nothing more to say. She was hardly one to give relationship advice, but she felt she must say *something* to comfort her sister. She told her that everything would be fine and that if he really liked her, he would be willing to talk. If not, so be it; not everything was meant to be.

The logic seemed to ground Claire, but she was still worried about losing him. Genevieve remembered thinking, S*o what if you do? What's so special about this guy?* Her sister was so young. Was that what it was like to be "young and in love"? *Was* it love?

They talked more about how to approach the situation. Genevieve told her not to make any rash decisions and suggested she journal, sleep on it, and see how she felt in the morning. Giving Ryan some space might make him realize how foolish he'd been to say what he'd said.

Claire agreed, said thanks. Then she added she was excited to see Genevieve next month during spring break. It would be Genevieve's first time flying out west to see Claire at her school. Their first adult vacation together, just the two of them.

When she was finished telling ghost Claire this part

of the story, Genevieve yawned and then studied her sister. It was hard to see in the dim light of the lamp. She'd been talking for so long, she forgot to turn on the lights as the sun set. Ghost Claire was hovering in the corner, a serene look on her face as she took everything in. Genevieve couldn't tell at all what she was thinking. How could she just stand there saying nothing about the breakup episode? The whole situation had clearly been a red flag, and Genevieve realized that she was now wanting some kind of explanation from Claire, or some kind of apology. But the ghost only offered maddening silence.

Genevieve yawned again, then announced she was going to bed early. The wine had made her tired, and she had work tomorrow, but it would be Friday, so afterwards they could hang out on the weekend. Then she laughed at the thought. Hang out doing what, exactly?

* * *

I say *Okay* and watch my sister get up woozily from the couch. I follow her around as she gets ready for bed, brushes her crimped hair, brushes her teeth, puts in the retainer she's had since she was 14.

She gets under the covers and sits in an upright

position. "So...do you just float around all night or what?"

"I sure hope so. I would love to go around the city. I'm not tired at all."

Genevieve yawns once more. "All right, well...good night, then." Her eyes are puffy from crying earlier, but she focuses them on me and stares. "I just can't believe you're here," she whispers. "It's really good to see you."

I smile. "You as well."

Gen falls asleep soon after that, and I float around her apartment. It's fun going through the walls. Though I had plans to go outside and float around the city, I find myself tethered to this place, and I can't seem to leave. Or, I realize, I don't really want to. I don't mind, though.

Around 3AM, I float back into Gen's room. She's sleeping on her back, head lolled to the side. She looks like a kid again. I am suddenly struck by a memory. It was a stormy night. The thunder felt like it was right above the roof. I was in my bed, and Gen was in hers. Any time the lightning flashed, I tensed. Gen wasn't asleep yet either. I told her I was scared and asked if I could sleep in her bed, and she said yes. We had narrow twin beds with a night table between us, but we were so small that we could easily fit in just one bed, so I climbed into Gen's and put my arm over her.

It was the only time that ever happened.

* * *

Genevieve's hangover really wasn't all that bad, but she took a Tylenol nonetheless. Her sister was nowhere to be seen, so she showered, dressed, and made some scrambled eggs with toast and tea.

As she moved the eggs around in the pan, she wondered if last night had been real. Maybe that's why her mom hadn't said anything about Claire being dead on the phone – because it was all in her head. That would explain a lot. Perhaps she'd entered an altered state of some kind. She didn't know whether to be concerned or impressed that her brain could hallucinate that clearly. It had felt so true.

And in her dreams last night, she'd walked sluggishly, like in slow-motion, down the road from her mother's house, her childhood home, and her sister had appeared – the real Claire, except she appeared as her seven-year-old self. Round face, freckled nose, shoulder-length hair partially pinned back with a barrette. Genevieve knew it was the real, living Claire because every time she saw her in the dream, she felt sad in a nostalgic kind of way. As if she knew in the dream that that little girl was gone forever. Seeing ghost Claire last night, though, hadn't

43

made her sad exactly; it had made her feel...loved.

Genevieve stopped stirring the eggs. She had certainly not been expecting that. But it was true. It was so comforting to see her sister again, even if she was a ghost. Something about the whole evening made her feel like everything would be okay.

And it would be, once she saw the real Claire on Sunday.

Genevieve scraped the eggs onto the toast. That was only two days away now. Her stomach did a flip-flop. Whatever happened would be okay. She knew she had to go into it with no expectations. No agenda. It may be the only chance she'd get in a very long time to make amends with her sister, the real version, in person.

Genevieve picked up her plate and tea, turned around and gave a little yelp, nearly dropping her breakfast.

* * *

"Don't do that!"

I grin and do a twirl. I'm standing right in the middle of the kitchen island, the black faux marble countertop meeting me just above my hips. "Look at my torso! It's completely cut in half." I don't feel anything as I move around the island.

"You scared me." Gen sets her stuff down at the breakfast bar. "I thought you weren't real. I thought maybe I hallucinated you last night."

"Nope," I reply. "I've been here the whole time. At least I'm pretty sure I have."

"How can you not know?" Gen bites into her toast.

"There's a lot we don't know," I reply. "The last thing I remember was watching you sleep at 3AM."

"M'kay. That's weird…"

"But now suddenly I'm here," I say, gesturing around the apartment. "I think it has something to do with you."

Gen chews for a moment, then asks, "What do you mean?"

I move out of the island and glide around to the other side of the breakfast nook. "Well, I wasn't able to leave the apartment last night. I just felt compelled, like it was my place to be here. Here, as in, wherever you are. And I think when you fell into a deep sleep, I ceased to exist until you thought of me again."

"So this *is* all just in my head. Great."

"No," I say slowly. "It's not that. It's something bigger. More important." I feel good about this deduction. I feel a purpose rising in me. "I am me, my own self. And also not. I am connected to you somehow, but also not. Gosh, I really cannot put my finger on it."

"The real Claire would never say *gosh*."

"I'm not the real Claire. I'm just all the pure, leftover bits of her."

"How do you know that?"

I pause. It's a good question. How *do* I know that? It just sort of came out. Maybe another ghost thing.

Oh, I know why. It's because of the bliss. That *goodness* enveloping me. That's still not the right word for it, though. I will have to answer her question when I have a better one, so for now I say, "I just do." It's not exactly untrue.

Genevieve isn't satisfied with this, but I leave her to finish her breakfast and get ready for work. She locks up her apartment and heads outside.

I follow her down the hall to the stairs, proving my theory that it's her I'm tethered to and not the apartment.

She pushes open the stairwell door. "I do hope I'm the only one who can see you. I would hate to have to explain all this," she says, gesturing to me.

"I guess we'll find out."

"Please don't scare the kids or act weird or anything. We have a full house today."

"As if I would."

I could easily just fall through the floor to the lobby if I wanted to, but I stick with Gen, acting as her shadow. Her haunting.

It becomes apparent immediately that no one can see or hear me except Gen. We ride the subway, and I take the opportunity to make faces at her from across the train car. The edges of her mouth twitch, and she tries to look away. But then I start making faces at other people as well.

A somber-looking woman stands like a zombie, holding on to the hang ring while I make a maniacal grin next to her face. A young dude sits with his legs spread open, eyes glued to his phone. I sit next to him, give him a cross-eyed look and yell, "Hey, close your legs!" When we reach the next stop and the exchange of people from train to platform and back happens, I over-exaggerate my actions to mimic a man lifting his briefcase, looking at his watch, letting out a sigh.

"Stop it," Gen whispers, stifling a laugh. The somber woman standing in front of her frowns and moves away.

Back up on the street, we pass some stray cats and a few dogs walking their owners. They bark and hiss at me, of course. Animals are so sensitive.

At the daycare, I watch as Gen gets to work. Work not being the operative word. She gets to play all day. In the morning she does arts and crafts, then some teaching time. Then lunch. Then before she does her marketing work on the computer, she brings out dolls of all sorts and plays make-believe with some of the toddlers.

A vivid memory comes back. The two of us in our room playing with Barbie dolls, setting up the Barbie furniture, deciding who gets which clothes and shoes. Picking out names for our characters and deciding the situation we wanted the story to begin in. It often followed the same scenario – both of our characters were always in college (because, of course, when we were little, we wanted nothing more than to be grown up), and they'd be getting ready to go to a party, but then something would happen. And it was usually something dramatic, like one of them finding a creepy message in her room, or while at the party, a guy (the Ken doll) might ask one of the Barbies out, and the other girl would get jealous. Or sometimes they'd pack up the Barbie RV (complete with a foldout bed, pop-up oven and plenty of cabinet space), and take it outside in the grass and drive them around, pretending they were in a jungle.

I was always the first to lose interest in these games. Gen didn't like that I would just suddenly change my mind and announce *I'm done* or *I'm tired*. I think she would have played forever if I'd not done that. I never understood why it was so important for me to be there. She could easily just continue the game without me. It was make-believe after all. Anything could happen. But now I think I know why she wouldn't – because it wasn't as fun once I left.

Sometimes, though, I had good reason to stop playing the game. Gen was too controlling. Too invested in what was happening. It was off-putting when she tried to control the narrative too much. They were just Barbies. I mainly liked playing with them for the shoes and outfits. She always wanted the stories to go somewhere, while I just wanted to play.

She's different now, though. Her only goal with the Barbies today is to keep the kids entertained, even if it makes no sense. There is no story, really. I watch as she takes the Barbie with long auburn hair and blue eyes, dresses her in a punk singer outfit, and puts her in the convertible, aimlessly pushing her around the carpet and making funny car noises, which makes the kids laugh.

* * *

The hours flew by. Ghost Claire hovered around all day but kept her promise. She didn't scare the kids with any weird poltergeist moves. Instead, she just watched

Genevieve and made faces at her from across the room whenever she caught her eye. Silly faces. Derpy faces. The ones Claire used to make at her when they were being total goofs for no reason other than the fact that they were sisters. She laughed out loud at some of them and had to make up lame reasons to her coworkers about *what was so funny.*

It was a good day. Genevieve felt things were promising, both about ghost Claire being here and the prospect of seeing the real Claire on Sunday. But as she sent the last kid home with their parents and locked up the daycare, said goodbye to her coworkers and headed for the subway, she felt dread. She still had lots to tell ghost Claire, and she suddenly felt like none of it mattered. Did ghost Claire really need to hear it? Couldn't the ghost version just stay with her as is, especially if things went bad on Sunday? She didn't know how these metaphysical things worked, and it rattled her nerves.

Suddenly, she didn't want to return home to the apartment. She wanted a drink and fresh air. Somewhere quiet. The park would be good. Genevieve ducked into a liquor store, then headed towards Albert Park. It was a lovely old park with walking paths that cut through, big red oak trees and benches dotted throughout. In the centre was a small fountain. She liked to go there sometimes and watch people. Decompress. Listen to a podcast until she got bored and needed human attention again. Then she'd either text her friend-with-benefits or a girlfriend, or her parents.

She took a seat on one of the benches and put in her headphones to make it look like she was on a call. Then, when no one was looking, she tipped some of the alcohol into her tea thermos and took a swig. She closed her eyes for a moment, feeling the autumn sun on her face, listened to the sound of the fountain's water, the eternal splashing. Welcomed the loosening feeling of the alcohol.

When she opened her eyes again, her sister's face was right in front of hers.

* * *

"Boo!"

Genevieve shrieks.

Some of the other people in the park shoot questioning glances in Gen's direction and I laugh.

"Ugh, don't do that," Gen says.

"Do you remember when we used to scare Dad all the time?"

"Yes. He hated it."

"And then you'd say it was my idea."

Gen shrugged. "Yeah, well, you were the baby. They were more likely to forgive you."

"Always the scapegoat."

Gen chuckles. "But, like, not in a bad way. Just as siblings, ya know?"

I do know what she means. I'd be lying if I said I never did the same to her or Peter. But it was the other way around more often than not.

"What are we doing out here?" I ask.

Gen takes a swig. "Didn't feel like going home just yet. And since I can't exactly take you to enjoy a night out at a bar, I figured this would do."

"I like it here." The trees are tall, the fountain is soothing. But I know we aren't here just to look at nature. After some polite, jovial comments to Genevieve about her job at the daycare – she really is better with kids than I thought she'd be – I get back to the matter at hand, the matter I know she wants to address. "So, what happened when you visited me during spring break that year?"

Gen sits cross-legged on the bench and wraps her coat around herself tighter. "Oh, it was sort of fun. But mostly totally bizarre. When I arrived, Claire – you – had already made up with Ryan, and it wasn't just you picking me up at the airport. He was there too."

"What was he like?"

"He was shyer in person than I thought he'd be. He kind of awkwardly hung back when you came to give me a hug. You were so giddy and overly excited for me to be there. I felt like you were putting on a show for him or something. I wanted to be happy for you, I really did. But I couldn't stop thinking about what he'd said to you before, when you'd called me crying." Gen takes another swig. "I thought it was just going to be me and you the whole week hanging out, going to shops and restaurants, meeting your friends, whatever. But he was constantly there. Well, there were a few times you did manage to get rid of him, and you took me on a tour around the city. That was really fun." Gen smiles. "We walked along the water where there were lots of people walking their dogs. One of them nearly knocked me over running for her ball. You mentioned how much you missed Sparky. I told you he was getting old but hanging in. You had been the one to pick him out as a puppy, so I think you felt bad about being away from him so much."

Gen takes another mouthful of her drink. "It was in those moments when we were alone together that I felt you were the person I had grown up with. We talked about all sorts of things, acted silly in our own way. You showed me some of your paintings you had done during school. You'd gotten so much better. I could see how you were evolving. But then you mentioned again how you hadn't really painted much since the fall. I remember thinking, something's wrong here. That's not the Claire I know. But you just carried on talking."

I float circles around Gen as she speaks, wishing I could remember our spring break visit. Wishing I could change it so that it wasn't so bizarre for her. It must be strange to have grown up with someone, to have shared a room with them until you were 13, to have shared clothes, ideas, stories, to have created so many inside jokes with them that other people got annoyed from being excluded, to have felt loved enough by them that it didn't matter how much you screamed yelled and hit them, they would still be there because they were your blood – it must be strange to have all of that, and then have an experience with them that caused you to doubt who you thought they were. At least, that's what I think Gen means when she says the trip was bizarre.

"There was one night we were watching a movie in your bedroom, and you were on your phone basically the whole time. I could see out of the corner of my eye every time your screen lit up with a text from someone. Halfway through the movie, you said you had to go to

Ryan's place. He needed help with something, but you said you'd be back later. Then you left." Gen shifted on the bench and took another swig. "As I sat there alone watching this dumb movie, I thought, would I do that if you were visiting me? Would I ditch you for some guy? I knew I wouldn't. So then I wondered why the hell you were being so clingy with him. What was so great about Ryan? Were you just being immature and naïvely in love? I really didn't know because I suddenly felt I didn't know my sister. I started to wonder if it was possible that Ryan knew you better than I did at that point." Gen snorted. "That's how weird it was. I was wondering if a guy who had known you for only three months might know something that I didn't about my sister. Suddenly, I was questioning…everything."

I hover in front of Gen. Her eyes are already starting to droop from the whiskey. I hope she doesn't get sleepy.

"Did I come back?" I ask.

Gen shakes her head and gives a forced laugh. "No, you didn't." Another swig. "So, I read your journal."

* * *

It's not something that Genevieve is exactly proud of, but she felt it was necessary. She herself had tried keeping a journal once when she was eight and then again at 12. But she was too lazy to write by hand and got bored easily. It felt like a chore, and her mind moved too quickly to indulge in such a thing. Claire on the other hand had always kept journals. She filled them up, too. Who knew what volume number she was on by that point. She was always very secretive about her journals, and for most of their childhood Genevieve had not peeked. Well, she tried once or twice of course but got caught, so Claire learnt to hide her diaries in better places.

The journal she was using at the time of Genevieve's visit, however, wasn't hidden particularly well. In fact, the teal soft-leather journal was just sitting out on her desk practically screaming to be read. Genevieve thought it may give her some answers, so while the movie was still playing and she was alone in Claire's room, she picked it up.

Claire's handwriting was swirly and cursive, just like her expressionist paintings, but it was legible enough that Genevieve was able to read several entries until she started to feel like she knew *too* much and set it back down.

In an entry dated February 23, Claire wrote that

Ryan had said it was really sad and in such poor taste that her parents had gotten divorced when they did. Couldn't they have waited until Claire was out of the house? He said he felt bad for Claire that she came from such a broken home with parents who had been so self-involved about how much they disliked each other. *He said it sounds like they put more energy into hating each other than they did into loving their kids, especially me. And he's so right. I was miserable during my last years of high school because of their stupid divorce. Could they really not have waited till I graduated and left? They waited just fine for Peter and Gen to leave, but clearly didn't care enough about me to do the same. Ryan said family is the most important thing to him, and if his parents ever got divorced he would just die.*

Genevieve flipped the page, cringing at how invasive Ryan's opinions were. Those were her parents too that he was talking about. What the hell had Claire been telling him? How bad a picture had she painted about their childhood? For as long as Genevieve had known her parents, she'd never experienced them to be very happy together for longer than several months. Peter was the only one who got to witness a time when they were in love and truly happy. He said it was when Genevieve was about two and he was seven that things started to crumble, but he didn't really know why. Then their parents learnt they were pregnant with Claire, and that, according to Peter, had temporarily brought some happiness back. But soon after Claire was born, the fights returned again, on and off, and it largely stayed that way until they were divorced.

But Genevieve didn't feel her childhood had suffered terribly because of it. They still had Christmases and treasure hunts and birthday parties and toys and dance lessons and went out for dinner and movies. Genevieve had always felt growing up that there was this universal understanding in their house that although Mom and Dad were not usually happy, it wasn't something to be talked about. It was just the norm. Once when Genevieve was six, she asked her mother if she and Daddy were going to get divorced, like all her other friends' parents were. Her mother had said, *Of course not, my little princess*, and that was that. Genevieve felt it to be true. She felt safe.

Maybe it had been different for Claire somehow. All of the weirdness between Claire and their parents after Ryan came on the scene – it couldn't all be because Claire's last two years of high school were uprooted at home, could it? Surely, Claire must have known their parents were headed for divorce anyway. What did it matter if they did it two years earlier than Claire felt they should have? Genevieve felt there was more to it, and she continued reading the journal, hoping to find the answer.

All the recent entries mentioned Ryan at some point or another, and they were always in praise of him. According to the journal, he took Claire to the studio one time and taught her about printmaking. She took him to the art museum and told him all about the paintings there. They got along "famously" at school. All their artsy friends treated them like they were the *It Couple*, and all her girlfriends were telling her how amazing she and Ryan seemed together. Claire was smitten and "happier than ever", apparently. She mentioned their parents a few more times, expressing frustration about how slow they still were to sing Ryan's praises. *It pains me to talk to them right now. Don't they want me to be happy?* At the time of reading that, Genevieve hadn't really thought much of it. All kids fought with their parents at some point or another, even well into adulthood. But once everything blew up between Claire and their parents, looking back on that journal entry, Genevieve now realized the weight it carried and wished she had taken it more seriously.

When she got further back into entries dated in the fall, right before meeting Ryan, Genevieve was surprised to find an entry where Claire mentioned going to see the campus counsellor. She was feeling stressed and sick to her stomach about having not only accepted a spot in the end-of-year art show, but also having agreed to help run and organize it. It would be the end of her third year, with one year left to go before graduation, and part of her fine arts degree in painting required an exhibition at some point. Genevieve remembered Claire telling her about it; the graduating students were invited to put on their own exhibition in an end-of-year art show, which was really more of a fair that took place on campus, showcasing all various mediums of art. It was usually full of fourth-year students' work. But Claire had been asked to fill a spot and get involved. How could she decline such an honour?

Genevieve remembered the day when Claire FaceTimed her to tell her the news. She was excited but also said how nerve-wracking it would be. It meant that from then until the show, she had to create several new works to exhibit. She hated creating work under pressure, though. That wasn't supposed to be the point of art, she'd said. Claire believed you were meant to do it when you felt inspired. Genevieve didn't see the problem; Claire was always inspired and never far from holding a paintbrush. But that day on the phone, she'd seemed worried. That must have been right around when she went to the counsellor.

Holding the leather journal in her hands, Genevieve wondered if she should have paid more attention around that time. She'd been dealing with her own issues of still trying to find a job after having graduated earlier that year. She'd had tons of interviews lined up, and although she was good at talking to people, she just wanted them to be over with. Had she complained too much about it to Claire that day on the phone? She couldn't remember. She just knew that Claire certainly hadn't mentioned anything about a counsellor.

Maybe that's what was so appealing about Ryan; he was a welcomed distraction. A reason to procrastinate. A new muse to focus on. The journal entry started to go into some depth about the experience with the counsellor, but it was at that point Genevieve decided to stop reading. She felt that whatever her sister had said in a confidential meeting with a professional therapist should remain that way. She returned the journal to its place and finished the movie. Claire still hadn't come back and hadn't texted. It was getting late by that point, and Genevieve was tired. She texted Claire to say she was going to sleep but got no reply.

The next morning while Genevieve was making tea,

Claire finally crept in, still wearing the same pyjamas as the night before. Her hair was a mess, and she had a sheepish look on her face. Genevieve remembered thinking that she looked like a kid still, and she felt minor disgust. What did Claire think she was doing, ignoring her older sister like that?

Genevieve didn't even want to ask what Ryan had so "urgently" needed help with, but something told her she was going to have to pretend to care.

* * *

Genevieve rubs her eyes with her palms, lets out a big breath. "I felt so embarrassed for you when you came in, like I was the parent, and should be telling you off or something. But I was there visiting for fun, so it also felt like it would be weird to say something."

None of this triggers any memory for me. I wonder why I was so dead set on Ryan at the time. "What did you do?" I ask.

"I just asked what happened. You said sorry for not texting, and that you hadn't realized how late it had gotten, and so you decided to just stay over because you didn't want to wake me if you came back in late and blah blah blah. Then you asked me how the movie was, trying to change the subject. I said it was fine, but why didn't you text? You said, 'I just told you why.' Then you went to get changed, and I finished making the tea. When you came back in, of *course* you just had to say, 'So aren't you even going to ask if everything's okay?'" Gen rolls her eyes and shakes her head. "I almost said, 'Yeah, is everything okay between you and me? Between you and Mom and Dad?' But I knew you were really referring to Ryan. So I said, 'Okay, what's wrong with Ryan? Is everything all right?' And then you didn't even give me a straight answer!"

I make a *tsk* sound. "How annoying."

"I know!" Gen takes another swig. "You suddenly got all vague and were like, 'Oh, he was just dealing with some personal stuff. Some anxiety and a minor panic attack. You know. He just really *needed* me, that's all. *He needs me a lot.*' Yeah, okay…" Gen shakes her head again, surveying the park as the sun falls behind the trees. Her breath visible in the crisp air. "It was so pathetic. In high school, I would have told you how stupid that sounded. You barely even knew this guy, and now he was your everything. But I felt like I couldn't say anything bad about him, because otherwise you might freak out. So I just said, 'Oh, okay. That sucks.'"

I smile because I'm reminded of a time when Gen did sort of tell me how dumb I was being about this guy

I liked in high school once. Tyler was his name. He was this quiet, sensitive musician. Tall, lanky, lame haircut, but I thought he was so cool and suave. He was shy too, but that just made him more attractive. He had also kind of started to show interest in me, but then there were rumours going around about him having a major crush on this other girl. I came home that day and whined to Gen about it. *What should I do? What do I say next time I see him?* Gen said *You're not even dating him! Who cares!* I remember feeling so hurt because she made me feel so stupid in that moment. I went off in a huff to my own room, and she to hers. Looking back on it now, I smile about it because it *was* silly, and it fills me with joy.

"What about the journal?" I say. "Did you ask her – me – about anything to do with what you'd read? Surreptitiously, of course." I drift around, moving back and forth through the empty spot on the bench beside Gen.

"In a way." Gen hugs her knees to her chest, takes another gulp. "The rest of the trip was…odd. Ryan was always there after that night, so I couldn't really ask you much, but one time when we were finally alone, I asked you what Ryan thinks about Mom and Dad. You hesitated, didn't meet my eye. Then finally you said that he really likes them and just wishes they would like him too. *They haven't been very welcoming towards him. I feel like they have something against him.* I tried to suggest that maybe it's because they don't really know him yet. At that point, they still had never met him in person. They'd only seen him on FaceTime a few times, plus there was that whole weird apology thing with Dad. You just waved a hand dismissively and said that wasn't enough of a reason. Then you went on to say how *his* parents had been super accepting and loving towards you already, as if it was a competition or something. Again, I tried to suggest maybe that's because they'd already met you in person. It was easier for them, as they only lived an hour away from the school. And you just kept saying, 'No, that's not it.'"

It's getting fairly dark by now, and Gen's hands are cold. I can tell because they look dry and cracked. But she's not shivering. I'm sure the alcohol is keeping her warm.

I wish I had something more to add to this story about Ryan, something to explain my behaviour, but I don't. "Come on, let's go somewhere else," I say, suddenly inspired to go do something. The bliss feeling surges, and I float a circle around her. Then I suddenly remember one of the worst songs I've ever heard in my life. In my cringiest voice I start singing the chorus of

"Friday".

Gen bursts out laughing. "Oh my God. So you remember *that* song but can't remember who Paul McCartney is?"

I shrug. "I don't make the rules."

Gen stands up, still chuckling. "That music video was so bad it was good."

I continue singing, plastering a big fake smile on my face and making awkward dance moves.

"Stop," Gen says, wiping her eyes, her shoulders jiggling.

She finally starts walking, and I float along beside her, the music video coming back to me in full force. It had been Gen who showed the video to me when I got home from school one day. Peter had sent it to her. I was always the last one to know about things.

But that's all in the past. Nothing really matters except that I'm here with Gen. "Where are we going, then?" I instinctively want to grab her arm and hook mine through it, but I know I can't. So I just smile and sing.

* * *

The girls spent the remainder of that night walking around the city. Genevieve felt confident enough from the liquor that she didn't even care if people thought she was strange, talking as if someone were right next to her. With her headphones still in, it was hard for anyone to surmise if she was really on a call or actually crazy.

Genevieve wanted to know what it was like being dead. What was it like to walk through objects? Ghost Claire told her to find out for herself and pointed to a pole. Genevieve laughed and the pole swayed in her vision. Then ghost Claire described the feeling of bliss that she'd mentioned before, and how she didn't think she was capable of feeling anything else. It was wonderful being a ghost, she said, and Genevieve admired her for being so lighthearted about it. She imagined she would be fearful to find herself in such a state. Had Claire always been this jovial in life? Genevieve surprised herself by immediately thinking yes; she'd just never noticed before. She looked at the ghost drifting a few steps ahead and wished she could go back. Appreciate her sister more when she had the chance.

As they passed by late-night cafés and folky restaurant bars, Genevieve wanted them to go inside, sit down, order some food and drinks. She felt a pang in her stomach, wondering if she'd ever get to spend time with the real Claire again.

Why was ghost Claire even there? Would she be

around forever now? Genevieve wondered if the real Claire would be able to see her own ghost on Sunday, or if it was just Genevieve who could see her. Claire had mentioned something last night about ceasing to exist once Genevieve fell into a deep sleep. Maybe something submerged within Genevieve had summoned this ghost version of Claire at a time when she really needed her. But it still made no sense because on Sunday, Genevieve was going to see the real Claire anyway. She felt another pang in her stomach, but more of a drop, an emptying.

It was the same feeling she'd had when she'd checked her messages all those years ago and realized her sister was unreachable. Her innards emptied. Her heart sped up. Had her sister really ended things? Genevieve's first thought was that it wouldn't last. Now she realized how naïve that thought had been. How hopelessly hopeful.

Especially after the email exchange from last spring. She would get to that, though, eventually. She didn't really want to tell ghost Claire about it because she was worried about how it would make herself seem. Then again, ghost Claire didn't seem to judge anything. She really was the purest version of Claire.

Claire. What if she was actually dead? Genevieve still hadn't heard anything in the news or from any other family members or the police. But suddenly it was all Genevieve could think about. The fact Claire's ghost was there didn't seem to be proof enough that she was really dead, but Genevieve didn't exactly have any proof that she wasn't *not* dead either. Maybe she was both. Schrödinger's cat. She had to know.

She pulled out her phone, her fingers shaking.

–What are you doing?

Genevieve ignored ghost Claire's question and looked up her sister's number in her contacts. She knew a trick that allowed her to get through to a blocked number. She turned off her caller ID, as she'd done before a few years ago on Claire's birthday, and the call went through. Her gut flip-flopped.

The phone rang, and after a few rings her sister answered. It was her all right. She said hello once, then twice. Genevieve's breath caught in the cold autumn air, her voice stuck in her throat, resisting the urge to burst forth. Then Claire hung up.

Genevieve's heart pounded. She had her answer, at least. She put her phone away, then looked over at the smiling ghost of her sister, who was still very much alive.

* * *

"Was that me?" I ask.

Genevieve nods. She's looking at me strangely like she's trying to piece everything together. She'll never figure it out, though, because even I don't know.

"Yep," she says.

"I thought you said I blocked you."

"You did. There's a trick to get around that. That's the second time I've used it."

I open my mouth in mock disgrace, trying to lighten the mood. "You've only tried calling me twice in the past five years?"

Gen puts her hands in her pockets and continues walking. "You don't understand. It's not exactly great continuously reaching out to your sister and being rejected every time. After numerous messages and emails, I finally tried to call you one day a few years ago after looking up how to call a blocked number. You answered then, too, but immediately hung up when I started talking."

I hover along beside her, passing right through a telephone pole. "I can't believe I would do that."

"Yeah, well, you did."

I think the booze is wearing off a bit. She seems less happy all of a sudden. "Why call me again now?"

"I just had to know. Is she really alive? Are you *not* her ghost? If not, then what are you?"

"I'm me," I say. "Your sister. And I resent being referred to as a what."

"Whatever."

A classic Genevieve response when she doesn't want to argue anymore. Though I'd hardly call this arguing. At least, I don't see it that way.

We move in silence for a minute before she says, "You know, Mom and Dad also tried calling you using the trick I just did. They got the same result as me. You hung up on your own parents. I even called Ryan one time. I don't know if he had me blocked or not, but I bypassed the caller ID just in case. I guess he was immediately suspicious when he saw it come up as *No Caller ID* because when he picked up, he didn't even say hello or anything. Just waited for me to talk. I could hear a shallow breath. I said, 'Hello, it's Gen', then he just hung up." Gen sighs, takes longer steps down the sidewalk. "There is nothing more frustrating to me than not being able to communicate."

"Oh, I know."

"Do you, though?" She shoots me a doubtful look.

"Please. I lived with you for 16 years."

I probably know better than anyone how much she hates not being able to communicate. When we were really little, I remember she was so frustrated once she cried just because I wouldn't say sorry for something I had done. I kept walking away, completely indifferent to whatever it was I had done, in my own little world. And all she wanted was for me to acknowledge my actions. She cried, pulled her hair, screamed into a pillow. I remember thinking she was crazy, a "total spaz" as my friends said to me the next day on the bus when I told them about it. It felt special, to be accepted by those kids on the bus. They "got" me, and that felt truer than giving in to my sister's demands. I'm sure she would have smacked me had Dad not come in and asked what all the fuss was about. In the end, he made us both say sorry to each other.

I ignored her like that sometimes because it was the only power I could wield over her when I'd had enough. She didn't act like it from the outside, but inside, Gen was just a deep well of emotions. She fell into that well often when our parents argued so much that they didn't have the capacity to deal with her in addition to their own problems. On those days when her communication with our parents was shut down, she'd turn to me. She'd vent about something. Yell at me. Cry because of whatever. She always insisted on being heard. Sometimes I was okay with it. Mostly, though, I just wanted to be alone and paint. I didn't like being sucked into her unhappy world. I had my own demons to deal with. I told her to go get a journal and talk to that. She told me that was a lame idea.

Gen turns a corner and I ask, "Where are we going now?"

She sighs. "Oh, I don't know. Home, I guess. I'm kind of tired."

I get the feeling Gen's lost her sense of fun nowadays, and I want to know more about how she's changed in the past five years. She seems weighed down, and not just from the drinking. When I was graduating high school, she was finishing second year, and I don't really remember what she took in school, but I vaguely recall that she used to love social outings. I'm struck with the memory of talking to her on the phone one day, hearing about how awesome glow-in-the-dark bowling was with her new college friends. Afterwards, they'd gone to the downtown core and stayed out till nearly 3AM. She was quite chatty in those days. Energetic. Lively. She seemed to draw people to her; every week she had a new friend to tell me about.

Now she was getting tired early in the evening, wandering the streets alone, talking to a ghost.

"What do you do for fun these days?" I ask. I don't even feel cold as we walk along the storefronts; I miss the feeling of wind on my skin.

"Good question." Gen pauses, like she's trying to think of an answer. "I don't really know. My weeks are all the same lately. I feel like I'm waiting for something. I don't know. I don't know what I'm doing with my life. You were always the talented one. The quiet artist. You were going places, while my only talent was being the loudest in the room and still managing to be unheard."

"Maybe you weren't saying the right things. Or you were saying them to the wrong people."

"Like you?"

I shrug. "Possibly. I was more thinking Mom and Dad."

"But you were my sister. They were our parents. We're all supposed to listen and be there."

I twist my mouth, float from side to side. "Why, though? There's such obligation with family and…maybe it's not always meant to be that way."

Gen snorts. "There we go. Now you're sounding more like the real Claire."

"I *am* the real Claire. And living Claire is *also* the real Claire."

"How do you know? It just doesn't make any sense."

I float in front of her. "Would you just trust me for once?"

She pauses, then walks right through me.

* * *

It wasn't even 8PM, and already Genevieve felt drained. The chill was settling in. The drink was wearing off. She realized she hadn't even had dinner yet, so now she was both tired and hungry. She felt if she waited long enough, though, she could lose the appetite and just go to sleep. She thought she'd be so happy tonight with Claire's ghost to talk to, but with all these questions about what she did for fun and why should family be obligated about anything...now she just felt miserable. Mainly because ghost Claire had reminded Genevieve how numb she was to her own life right now. Sure, she had a full-time job at a well-established daycare (certainly not something she ever envisioned for herself), and she had a handful of friends she saw a few times a month, but she wasn't particularly close to any of them. And while she loved looking after the kids, the job was pretty boring, and the parents were largely assholes to deal with. The same thought had been rattling around in her head for months now: is this it? Is this all there is? Numerous failed romances, a failed sister relationship, her parents' failed relationship, failed relationships at work.

Once while walking to work, she saw a big yellow bus picking up a group of young kids, and a boy, maybe about 11, came running down the sidewalk. His knapsack was bouncing on his back, and he carried his coat as if he hadn't had time to put it on. Bless him, he was running so hard to catch his bus to make sure he got on, and all Genevieve could think was, *Poor kid, he doesn't even know it's not worth it.* School doesn't teach you anything you really ought to know in life. Here was another kid getting sucked into the system, and her eyes had welled up at the sight of him. She'd kept walking, and the bus passed her by.

She should know, having a degree in marketing and communications. It was the practical thing to do, and it was something she was good at. But she couldn't find a job because they all required two years of experience. The daycare needed extra carers, plus someone to run their marketing and Facebook group. Genevieve kind of fell into the job by accident, and she did it all, practically with her eyes closed.

That's what life felt like right now – one big closed eyelid. What did she do for fun? Tried to keep the lid open, depending on the day.

At least Claire had pursued what she loved, but even that didn't work out. Towards the end of the spring break trip, Genevieve asked what Claire was working on for the end-of-year art show. They were sitting on a patio having brunch. It was the day before Genevieve was due to fly back home. Claire bit into her croissant, chewed for a long time before answering. Then tried to change the subject. Genevieve asked again. This really wasn't like Claire to avoid questions about painting. What was wrong with her?

I'm not doing it, she'd said. *I gave my spot to Ryan. But* don't *tell Mom and Dad.* Genevieve was gobsmacked. People didn't just throw away something they've loved for over 10 years, not without any good reason. What was so damn good about Ryan Matar? He was just a guy. Claire went on to say that she was still helping organize the show, but Ryan was starting up his passion for printmaking again, and he was feeling anxious about telling his parents. *So stressed. He was barely sleeping.* He was worried he'd let them down unless he could really prove to them that he could make a go of it. Claire saw a way to help him, said he needed her spot in the art show more than she did, an opportunity she'd been working towards since she was 12. He needed it more.

Like hell Genevieve wasn't going to tell their parents.

Genevieve asked if it would affect Claire's school credit or anything like that. *Ugh, you sound just like Mom and Dad,* Claire had said, stirring her tea. She went on to explain that because she was a third-year student who had been asked especially, there was always next year for her, which was when she was technically supposed to do it anyway. Genevieve didn't understand. *But Ryan's a third-year! What's so special about him? How did they agree to this?* Claire said she'd persuaded them. Genevieve was stunned. So not only had Claire said, *Here, have my spot,* she'd *fought* for him to have it. This boy whom she'd only known for five months tops.

Part of Genevieve wondered if Claire was doing it out of spite, an effort to prove to their parents, and even Genevieve and Peter, that they were all wrong about Ryan. That they would be sorry they ever disliked him once they saw how amazing his exhibition would be in the show. Or maybe Claire was trying to prove something about herself, that she was more than just her art. Maybe this was payback for all the times Genevieve and Peter hadn't taken Claire seriously or had poked fun at her outfits, or for all the times Mom and Dad had said, *Clean up that paint mess in the basement.* Or maybe it was just a hard truth that Claire had turned into a guppy of a young woman, doing things for the approval of a guy.

Genevieve did not want to believe that, but she couldn't exactly claim that she hadn't done the same thing either at times. In her sister's case, though, she was worried how far Claire would take it. She seemed so unlike herself.

For weeks, Genevieve sat on this new information about the art show. She really did try to keep it in, but only because Claire had promised she would tell Mom and Dad soon. In April, though, they were still none the wiser and had each bought their own tickets to fly out in May for the art show. Being divorced made them far more civil towards each other, and they were actually able to do things – not together but parallel each other – without so much as a raised voice. Visiting their daughter's art show was one of those things.

Genevieve couldn't wait anymore. She told Claire their parents had bought tickets – when was she going to tell them? *Soon! Geez, calm down.*

That was it. Genevieve called them up right away and told them.

* * *

My eyes widen. "What did they do?"

We were back at the apartment now. Gen managed to sidestep my question about why she's so miserable in

79

life, so I asked her about what happened the rest of the spring break trip. She seems content to have something else to focus on. Except now she is collapsed on her couch, threatening to fall asleep.

"They were pretty livid. It was all a big mess. You were pissed at me. I was mad at you. Our parents were *so* disappointed and kept lecturing her over the phone. Then they said they would still come and at least see her, and they could finally meet Ryan too. But you told them no, *do not come.* You said not to bother because you didn't really want to see them anyway, given how they were reacting."

Gen rubs her eyes with her palms. I try to imagine seeing my parents now and what it would be like. I would want to see them, of course. As a ghost, I have nothing against them. I know they did their best.

One thing I would love to know, though, is why they fought so much. I never really knew why. I suppose being a kid, though, that's not something I would have understood anyway.

A memory surfaces: Dad sleeping downstairs on the couch for a whole month. Not because Mom said he had to, but because he chose to after their last argument. I remember going downstairs for a glass of water one night and seeing him there. Far too big for just an average living room couch, snoring, foot hanging off. I remember thinking, was this *his* part of the house now, and did Mom have to knock before entering? Was their bedroom now *her* part of the house, and would he have to ask permission to get his clothes? So many of my friends at school had broken families: separated parents, divorced parents, single parents, every-other-weekend parents. I was glad, proud even, that my family was one of the few left that was still intact, at least from the outside. What would I say if I had a sleepover at my place and my friends saw my dad sleeping on the couch? That's what I wondered as I drank my water that night from a red sippy cup.

It would be nice to see them now. It's been so long, even though I have no sense of time where I'm from; I just feel my memories of them are far away. I'm not even mad at them anymore, about the timing of their divorce. I accept they did what they had to with what limited knowledge they had of themselves and each other at the time. Doesn't mean they were right, but it couldn't be helped. The bliss feeling bubbles inside me.

Gen sighs. "I'm going to bed soon."

"First, tell me what happened. At the art show."

Gen rolls onto her side, stretches out on the couch. "I really don't want to get into it right now. It's...not good."

I raise a brow. "Has any of this been good?"

A pause. "Fair point." She curls up tighter on the couch. "But this is, like, extra bad."

"Well, now you *have* to tell me." I feel it's important for Gen to get all of this out in the open. She can't stop now just because it's getting worse.

"Are you sure you want to know? You kind of did something that makes you look really..."

"Really what?"

She doesn't answer, and this makes me bristle. I feel a sense of unease descend over my presence. Not much of what Gen has told me about myself up to this point has been "good" exactly, but what else could I possibly have done that was so bad it warrants hesitation from her?

"Come on. Tell me," I say.

No response.

"Gen!"

She groggily sits up on the couch. "It doesn't matter. It's not like it will change anything."

"Why are you being so evasive?"

"Because you couldn't handle it."

"How do you know what I can handle now?"

"Because you couldn't handle it then!" Her eyes are

reddening now, and she brushes at them irritably. "And I'm pissed at you for doing all the things you did and for not confiding in me and trusting me. And I know you're not the 'real' Claire," she says, "but I don't know how you're going to react, and you're, like, the best parts of the Claire I know. The happier parts and the goofy parts, and I don't want to ruin that. Why do you have to know any of this anyway? It doesn't change anything."

I suddenly realize she's trying to protect me from whatever bad thing I did. I soften and float down to her level.

"Please," I say. "I have to know what I did so that I can make you feel better."

"But I can't make *you* feel better," she replies. "I don't know why you did what you did, so I can't explain things. It's…awkward."

I think I know what she means, but now Gen's eyes are closing, and she is clearly about to pass out, so I let her.

The floor lamp is still on and I sigh. I try to turn it off, but I can't grasp the chain. I can't even feel it. My hand goes right through. I can feel the electricity, though. If I run my hand through the bulb, I get a slight tingly feeling in my palm. I spend about an hour making the lamp flicker as I run my hand through it, trying to turn it off. Then finally, out of nowhere, everything goes dark.

I must be getting stronger, but I don't know if that's a good thing or bad.

* * *

This time, Genevieve did have more of a hangover than she would have liked. Her mouth was dry, and her stomach rumbled, reminding her she hadn't had any food the night before, and now she had a headache too. Claire was nowhere to be seen, so Genevieve got up from the couch, drank three glasses of water, took a Tylenol and jumped in the shower.

One more day, and then she'd get to see her sister again in the flesh. She kept telling herself it was okay to go see her. She wasn't doing anything wrong. She had to try. Even after everything, all the arguing and back-and-forth, after ultimately blocking Claire's emails herself, Genevieve still had to try with an opportunity like this, right? She had this fantasy scenario in her head that the moment Claire saw her older sister in person, she would break down, she would feel *something* for Genevieve again. She would remember their bond. It wasn't the same when you sent an email or tried to call someone.

That was too easy for a person to walk away from. But in person, it was different. There was nowhere to hide.

What would Genevieve do, though, if Ryan was right next to Claire? That might ruin everything. Genevieve wasn't sure if she could hold her tongue in front of him. But the whole situation wasn't entirely his fault. Claire had still made decisions, at the end of the day. At first, Genevieve really did believe Claire's estrangement was entirely his doing, that he had tricked Claire into abandoning her family. But over the years, Genevieve began to think that it had to be Claire's own choice to go this long without attempts to make amends. Because how else would Claire do anything in life if she wasn't thinking for herself about this?

Genevieve wiped the fog off the mirror and gasped. Ghost Claire's pale face hovered behind her. She had that baby-faced expression: small mouth stretched into a slight upturned smile, her eyes bright and wide. It was exactly the kind of face Claire used to make whenever company visited the house. She'd act all shy and wide eyed around the adults. Genevieve used to think it was so childish, Claire acting so helpless. But she *was* helpless. She was just a kid, her little sister.

Genevieve was always talkative when aunts and uncles and grandparents came to visit, always so animated and goofy, and she supposed they thought that was cute too. But she felt they thought that Claire's quiet and shy baby-faced expression was cuter. Especially the way her chin-length brown hair framed her face at the time. During dinner, Genevieve always had to sit with Claire at the "kids' table", but Peter got to sit with the older cousins at the adults' table. Claire always seemed okay with this, such a happy-go-lucky child. But Genevieve got to a certain age where she didn't want to sit with the babies anymore.

–Look what I can do.

Ghost Claire floated up to the ceiling and whipped her hand through the lightbulb, causing it to extinguish, then turned it back on. Genevieve was confused. She didn't know what it meant, the fact that Claire's ghost was gaining abilities to turn lights on and off. Was her presence in this realm becoming solidified? Or was it something all ghosts could do if they put their minds to it?

Whatever the answer, her ghostly sister seemed so joyful this morning, even after their little spat last night. Genevieve's stomach flip-flopped. She wasn't sure how she was going to continue the story of the art show. She'd woken up and realized as much as she wanted to, she couldn't withhold information from ghost Claire about her own actions. She had every right to know. But it didn't mean it would be easy to hear.

* * *

"You need to eat," I say. I may be a ghost, but my hearing still works. Genevieve's stomach growls again.

"I know," she says. "I feel weak."

I follow her into the bedroom, where she gets dressed in black jeans and a cozy mustard sweater. Her ash-blond hair contrasts nicely with it.

"How are you able to turn off lights now?" she asks.

"I figured it out last night. Not much else to do."

"Is it a…good thing? Aren't you *not* supposed to be tangible?"

I shrug. "Who can say? Let's go get breakfast."

I'm feeling lively today, even after our little moment last night. Everything's harmonious and meant to be. I just know it. I want to know more about Gen's life. I have no idea how much time I have here, or what it means that I'm here, I just know that I've missed out on my sister's life, and I want to experience as much as I can with her.

Gen puts on her coat and grabs her bag. "We can go to my favourite place. You'll like it."

Something else pops into my head. In the hallway I

ask, "Do you remember when we were kids and you always said you didn't want kids, but I knew I was going to have probably two, and so we agreed that you would be the cool, crazy aunt?"

Gen smiles. "Ha. Yeah, I do remember that. We had this silly scheme that we would live close enough to each other that our houses could be connected by a pathway. And I would have horses and a cool farm, and you'd have the kids, and when you got sick of them, you could just send them down the path to my place."

"Auntie Gen's."

Gen gives me a look that makes me imagine my gut would pang, if I had one. She pushes the door open, and we step out. It's a bright blue fall day.

"I don't know what she's going to tell them," she says.

"Tell who what?"

"Your kids, if you ever have any." Gen puts her sunglasses on. "One day, they'll ask you where you come from, where your mom and dad are, and if you have any siblings. What are you going to say? That you just appeared on Earth out of the blue, fully formed?"

I grin. "Well, that *is* how I got here. And I am Claire, technically."

Gen gives me a look, a deadpan one I'm sure, from

behind her glasses. "But seriously," she says. "One day, I'll have a blood relative out there – maybe I already do, a niece or nephew – and I won't even know about it. Does she really hate us that much that she would do that?"

I follow along next to her as we turn a corner. She isn't even wearing her headphones anymore. Only a few people give her strange looks as she talks to thin air, but she seems unconcerned about anyone else today, except me.

"All I can say is that *I* would never do that to you," I say. "I would want you in my life. I would want to go to Bali with you. I would want you to babysit my kids. I would want to be able to call you up whenever, just so I could vent about something stupid. I would want to give you one of my paintings for your birthday every year. August fourth." The date suddenly pops into my mouth.

"You remember," Gen says with a smile.

"Yes," I say. "Sometimes things just randomly come back to me."

Gen stops in front of a narrow café entrance that has a tall pane of glass with *The Copper Kettle* hand drawn onto it from the inside. She sighs and says, "It's a nice thought, to know that you would still want to do all those things. But it almost doesn't matter, ya know?

You're not you. Not really."

"Maybe I'm not exactly the Claire you last knew," I say, "but I am the part of Claire that is still your sister." I know this to be true. And I know it's unimportant, the fact that I'm not the living Claire. I feel now that it's imperative Gen understand this, that I'm exactly who she needs Claire to be. That bliss feeling swirls around inside me again, validating my thoughts.

"I guess," she says. "But this is exactly why I need to see the real you tomorrow. To try to remind her this is how she was." She gestures to me. "This is the closest we've geographically been in…years. I need to at least try to create a future in which she would tell me when she's having a baby."

She smiles at me, then heads inside the café. She seems so certain about this meeting tomorrow. So much hope and expectation rides on it.

She's always done that. It's one of her blessings, always seeing the best in others, the prospects, the potentials, no matter how pessimistic she may get now and then. Though I could be a cheery kid, I was less optimistic most of the time, or maybe it just appeared that way because I kept to myself and my journals a lot. But she was always so open about situations. So determined to make things work.

It was also her downfall, though, because when something inevitably didn't work out, she would be crushed. I'd say, "Told ya!" Which she hated even more.

Another memory: Mom and Dad promising we'd go out to a movie and dinner one weekend. They were trying, they really were. I must have been about eight. Gen was so excited for the movie. We hadn't been out together as a family in ages. When she, Dad, and I went grocery shopping that day, she told Dad to buy the stringy liquorice. That was Mom's favourite, but they never had them at the concession stand at the movie theatre. Gen told him if they got it, Mom could sneak it in with them. He agreed and put the bag of red liquorice string into the cart. But Mom and Dad argued when we got home. Why hadn't Dad gotten the fresh salmon like it said on the list, instead of frozen salmon, and does she have to do everything herself around here. Dad said she was exaggerating. She said she wasn't in the mood anymore for a movie. She stayed home, told Gen to leave her alone. Gen didn't even show her the liquorice. She just hid it deep in the pantry and crossed her arms in the theatre while Peter and Dad ate popcorn and I stuffed my face with chocolates.

As the years passed, I feel like her anger rubbed off on me, and we swapped emotional places. She got happier when she left for college. I became sadder, alone in our house with our parents' storm. I wish we could swap places again now. Wish I could give her this bliss feeling I've been carrying around. Wish she could understand that this coming together tomorrow between her and Claire is not really what's important. I'm not sure why it's not important, I just know suddenly for the first time, undoubtedly, that it won't make her as happy as she thinks.

* * *

Once Genevieve had a warm mug of latte in her hands and a breakfast sandwich in her stomach, she felt the life returning to her.

She needed to stop drinking. She knew that much. It had gotten out of hand recently. It was too easy to do when she was feeling overwhelmed or numb. Letting go of this habit would be the first thing she'd change after she connected with Claire tomorrow. Then she really should get a haircut. Her pale hair had split ends, and the layers had lost their shape. She also needed to start looking for jobs again. The daycare was becoming scarily comfortable. It had been 13 months already since she'd started there. She could imagine telling Claire a few months down the road where her new job was and what the people there were like. And Claire would tell her what she was up to in her own life; maybe she'd even invite Genevieve for a visit. It would be good to put this all behind them. She wanted it to be tomorrow already. She felt this fantasy future was a castle made of paper, and it could easily be blown down in the next 24 hours. Now that the castle was there, she wanted to go towards it and waste no more time. Changes were coming. She had to believe it.

Ghost Claire sat across from her at the table, mouth pinned in a small smile, so serene looking as she watched Genevieve sip her latte. Genevieve's stomach did another flip. She wanted to start speaking, to tell ghost Claire the rest of the story, but her voice felt caught. She sipped her latte, relishing the warm, spiced elixir. Claire waited patiently, and the two sisters sat in silence for a while as Genevieve finished her drink.

Finally, she began talking. She started with the easier stuff. After Claire had told their parents not to come to the art show, their parents were beyond disappointed. Their father was furious, and in a huff he cancelled his flight and got his money back because he always bought tickets with the extra protection on them. Their mother, however, had not bought the extra protection, and she'd be damned if she was going to let her daughter speak to them that way. So she kept the flight but did not tell Claire she was still coming. She surprised Claire by showing up a week before the art show.

At this point, Genevieve put her mug down and made it clear to ghost Claire that she hadn't been there in person for this part of the story, and had only heard it from their mother's point of view. But, she added, she didn't see any reason for their mother to lie or exaggerate.

Ghost Claire only looked on serenely. Patiently.

Genevieve went on to tell her that Claire and their mother argued on the first day, but then things seemed to calm down, and they went out for dinner. Their mother explained to Claire that all she wanted was to support Claire in her aspirations and career, and she just couldn't understand how Ryan fit into it all. *I didn't sign up to pay for some other family's child to take over my daughter's place,* she'd said to Genevieve later on while recounting the story to her, sipping a Merlot.

When their mother finally did meet Ryan the next day, she said it had gone just fine. At least, so she thought. *I didn't like him, of course*, she'd told Genevieve. *But I thought we had an engaging adult conversation about art and politics.*

Genevieve knew, though, what their mother could be like when testing people. She was a force to be reckoned with, stubborn and opinionated. Genevieve shuddered to think what Ryan, a mere 21-year-old boy, might have been up against, meeting Mama Bear, as it were. But at the same time, Genevieve believed that no matter how their mother had come across, nothing she'd done could have warranted the treatment from Claire and Ryan that she'd received. Or rather, that Claire had allowed to happen.

Genevieve must have paused too long because, just then, ghost Claire reached her translucent hands across the table and wrapped them around Genevieve's, which were clamped around her mug. An ever-so-slight chill enveloped Genevieve's skin. Claire looked her in the eye and said the two words Genevieve had been wanting to hear for five years.

* * *

"I'm sorry," I say to Gen. "I'm really, really sorry for everything that happened."

Gen's shoulders visibly soften, and her eyes well.

"I know my memory is shot," I continue, "and I know I'm just a ghost, but I am Claire. And I apologize, for everything I said and did. Every way in which I mishandled things." I shrug. "Things get said, things happen, we lose control, and it's hard to come back from that, but not impossible. I was so young at the time. I don't know what living Claire will do with the rest of her life in regards to you or our parents, but I do know a part of her, the part that is me perhaps, is very sorry. She – I – never wanted any of this to happen."

I have to steady my hands over hers, since I can't actually feel where hers begin and mine end. I know she can feel me, though. The energy. Gen holds my gaze for a few moments.

"Thank you. I really needed to hear that," she says. She wipes the inner corners of her eyes and sits back in her chair. "You do know that I love you, right? Even with all of our fights, all the times we've hit each other, all the times I've ever called you gross or stupid or annoying. Even after everything." She motions around the café, but I know she means the last five years. "Even after how you treated us and how things fell apart, even after you chose Ryan over me, over any of us – I could never really hate you, or wish to never see or hear from you again. I could never really say that and mean it."

I smile at her, and I know those are the words she wants to say tomorrow, to the real Claire. I hope it's enough that she can say them to me now. "I know," I reply.

We're sitting at a two-person table at the back of the café near the washrooms. Genevieve sits facing the back wall to avoid being seen talking to herself. I don't have the heart to tell her that it makes no difference; the lady in the next table next to us her has been giving her the side-eye for the past five minutes.

Gen decides to order another latte, and while we wait for it to be served, she sighs, meets my eye and says, "Are you sure you really want to hear this?"

I take in her question, try to feel its answer within me. I think back on all she's told me so far. My actions, the things I said five years ago. It certainly doesn't paint me in a great light, but it's hard to relate to that because it's not like I can do anything about any of it. It all feels like it happened to someone else. I sink into my presence, the calm within me, the bliss, and all I feel there is love for my family. I do love them, all of them. Gen loves me. She just said so. She still loves me even after whatever it is she's about to tell me I did. And because of that, I know I can take it.

"Yes," I reply. "You don't have to understand it in order to tell me. Neither do I. And you don't have to worry about me hearing it now. I trust you."

Gen smiles back at me just as the barista drops off

her fresh latte. She begins to speak.

* * *

Genevieve's mother said that she asked Ryan about his printmaking ambitions, his family, his background, and any other interests he might have. *Just a normal conversation*, she'd said to her eldest daughter.

The three of them had made pleasantries as they sat in the kitchen of Claire's shared rental. Ryan told Claire's mother that his interests in art and printmaking stemmed from his father's Lebanese roots, which were rich in culture and art, especially folk poetry, song, and dance. Ryan was a quieter guy, though, and had always loved the more visual aspects – mosaics, paintings, murals, prints, photography, and other rich artworks that flooded the Middle East.

Genevieve's mother chimed in at that point about the rich cultures and artwork of Europe, too. She told him she was a bit of an "art nerd" as well, and that she'd visited the Louvre, countless galleries in London, art markets in Italy, and all sorts of auctions and other exhibitions during her travels. Growing up, she'd dreamt of studying art history and learning how to paint, but her parents never supported her enough to go to school. She then went on to tell Ryan that she had not been to the

Middle East yet and did not think it was safe to visit due to the political climate, various attacks, and even kidnappings.

Ryan pointed out that North America and many other places also have similar things going on all the time. Violence did not discriminate, and besides, he'd said, it wasn't like that everywhere in the Middle East. He recommended some safer areas for her and Claire's father to check out someday.

This got them talking about politics and all that had been happening in the news with civil unrest, riots, and the refugee crisis. Genevieve could just imagine how her mother would have tried to govern the conversation and one-up Ryan any time he said something. She couldn't be certain that that's how it *had* gone because, of course, her mother would never admit such a thing, but Genevieve had seen it before at times her mother was talking to someone whom she felt threatened by. If that was how things had gone, part of Genevieve could understand why Ryan might have found the conversation so off-putting, but it still didn't excuse Claire's behaviour afterwards. And Genevieve knew it wasn't entirely her mother's fault that she was the way that she was. In fact, both of her parents had their own demons from their younger years; lord only knew what was still left unaddressed and how it had manifested in their own offspring.

At that point in the conversation, Ryan said he was interested in creating political art. He wanted to do something with his printmaking in Lebanon and Syria that would get people thinking, challenge the dictatorship, bring awareness to the economic crisis, make a statement. He believed art was one of the most powerful ways to incite change for the better. *I simply disagreed*, Genevieve's mother had said with a shrug. *I felt his thinking was a bit naïve, and told him as much. I can have an opinion, can't I?*

Her mother went on to tell Ryan that perhaps his efforts would be best and more realistically put to use if he could do something more tangible to help, like vote. Did he have dual citizenship? If not, what about actually going there to volunteer at refugee camps and help people directly? Or even organizing an art fundraiser and donating the money to Lebanese non-profits. *All I said was that his dreams of making political art might be too lofty a goal. I was just trying to ground him a bit, that's all.* Genevieve understood her mother's line of thinking, and she knew she wasn't intentionally trying to tear him down, but clearly that's how Ryan must have felt.

Genevieve herself was torn because she could see

both sides playing out, even though she'd only heard her mother's side of it. She could understand how this type of conversation might rattle someone as young and hopeful as Ryan was, especially if he lacked confidence in any way.

But didn't Ryan realize that Claire's mom was just testing him? There he was, sweeping her baby girl off her feet and away, like he'd been doing so since before Christmas. And Claire's mother felt suspicious about it all. Her daughter simply hadn't been the same since meeting Ryan. Her motherly spidey senses couldn't stop tingling. She was feeling defensive, protective, cautious, *and I simply had to see what all the fuss was about. I had to be sure.* Anyone could understand that.

Ryan went home that afternoon and soon sequestered Claire with an urgent text. She told her mother she'd be back later, and indeed she returned much later that night, but something was off. Her mother sat on the living room couch reading the paper on her iPad. She asked Claire, *What's wrong honey? Where have you been?*

Claire was quiet, lips drawn tight, downcast gaze hidden between the curtains of hair that were so similar to her mother's. She held typed up pages in her hands. They was from Ryan. *Please don't say anything until I'm finished.*

Genevieve's mother could not believe it. *I felt ambushed,* she'd said to Genevieve, pouring more wine for herself. Her own daughter and her daughter's boyfriend were accosting her in the living room of Claire's rental suite, except the boyfriend hadn't even had the gall to show up in person, and instead sent a five-page letter in his place.

The letter described how inferior Claire's mother had made Ryan feel earlier. His parents had grown up poor; that's one of the reasons they chose to only have one child, Ryan's letter explained, and they couldn't afford to go to fancy museums or buy art materials when he was a kid. His father was a hardworking man originally from Lebanon, who had come to Canada and met Ryan's mother. By making Ryan feel like "garbage" – as Claire's mother had apparently done – he felt it was a personal attack on his parents, too. And his family's background. An undue judgement.

His letter further explained that he had issues from his past. Mental health problems. Social anxiety since he was a child. But he didn't expect her to understand any of that. Perhaps, though, she could educate herself before talking to someone who is known to have severe reactions – panic attacks, specifically – to microaggressive behaviour. He was bullied as a kid, he claimed, and was a very sensitive person. But of this he was proud. He liked to channel his sensitivity into art, and he knew it could make a difference. He didn't appreciate his dreams being squashed by his girlfriend's mother during their first meeting, when she – Claire's mother – hardly knew anything about him or what his artistic ideas and intentions were. More people could learn to be more sensitive, he said. *People like you.* It was a miracle that someone as lovely and thoughtful and caring as Claire had come from a family that practiced the opposite, he explained. In his culture, family relationships and personal connections were highly valued, but he could see that wasn't so within Claire's family. He didn't even want Claire's parents to meet his own. It would be *too embarrassing*, and he predicted they *wouldn't get along anyway, so why bother.*

Claire went on reading the five full pages of Ryan's saga, and whenever her mother opened her mouth to retort something, Claire's hand shot up with a silencing gesture. By the end of the letter, Claire was crying, her mother was crying, *and then she just ran out the door. Didn't even give me a chance to speak.*

After Genevieve's mother finished telling the story, Genevieve's dad, who had been sitting quietly at the table with them, taking it all in, finished his own wine and said he just couldn't believe it. How could Claire do that? What was she thinking? It was ridiculous. All of it. *That boy is ridiculous.*

He then went on to suggest to his ex-wife that maybe she'd made a mistake in going. Maybe it had made things worse. Maybe she should have hung back like Claire had wanted them to. Genevieve didn't think that was a very tactful thing for her father to bring up at a time like that, but he might have been right. Her mother shot back at him that he wouldn't understand her decision to go because he was a man. *It's different when you're a mother. I couldn't not go.* They began arguing again, just like the old days, and Genevieve's dad sulked off back to the safe haven of his little bungalow. Genevieve downed her wine.

Her mother finished off by saying that Claire spent the rest of the trip staying at Ryan's place. She begged her mother not to come to the art show on the final day, but she did anyway. His booth, Genevieve's mother claimed, didn't even have that much to show for, and what was there *wasn't all that good.* She didn't stay long, just enough to see what exactly her daughter had given up her space in the show for. *A total waste.* Then she flew back home.

HER SISTER'S GHOST

It was the last time she saw her daughter in person.

* * *

As I've been listening to Gen's story, the noise of the café has dimmed further and further into the background. I feel like I'm there, in the rental suite, having an out-of-body experience watching myself read a letter to my mother from my own boyfriend. It all sounds like it's about a version of me from some parallel world. I know I could be distant growing up, off in my own painted imagination. I know Gen struggled to express herself to our parents and often took it out on me. I know that sometimes I felt my parents saw me as an afterthought, too consumed by their own dislike for each other to notice when I needed them. But had I really been so unheard in my own family that I would latch on so willingly to the first sign of a way out? Was Ryan really even the way out for me? Or a way in to something that I'd been missing out on? It's difficult to arrive at an answer because I've never met this Ryan fellow. Nothing about this story stirs any memories for me. I feel so at peace, even after, or perhaps because of, hearing this harrowing tale. It's a missing piece to some puzzle that I can't quite make out yet. Nothing that Gen has told me feels out of place. Everything happens because it's meant to.

Genevieve crumples her napkin and puts it on her empty plate. She sips her latte and sits back in her chair. "So," she says, "what do you think?"

I study her face. Her hazel eyes bore anxiously into me. Her brows knit together in wrinkled concern. She's expecting me to feel terrible, but joke's on her. I'm stronger than I look. Although, "I have to admit, I wasn't expecting that. The letter part."

"I know, right? We were all surprised."

"It is a shocker, but…" I don't know how to explain it. I can't exactly tell her that it *doesn't* matter, because obviously it does matter to her, but at the same time, it's something that happened five years ago. I wonder how living Claire has changed since then. I wonder if she regrets reading the letter to Mom. All I know is that even though everything seemed horrible at the time, I know that no one did anything out of malice. There's so much more to it than that. All I can say is, "It's a shocker, but I have compassion for her. For me. But also for Mom."

"What do you mean?" Gen says, propping her elbows on the table.

"There was just…" I struggle to search for the

correct words. "…such a misunderstanding." Yes, this is it. I feel this seed growing fast within me. I grab the thread and follow it, looking back at all Gen has revealed, and all that is to come. "Every single thing you've told me has all just been a series of misunderstandings. No one has properly communicated throughout this entire thing. Not truly. And, if we can accept that, how can we possibly make a judgment call?"

Gen frowns. "So you're saying you're not taking sides because there's no sides to take? Come on, you have to have *some* sort of opinion about it all. About your actions with the letter."

"I do, and that was my opinion. I just told you."

"But it's a non-opinion."

"No, I said I have compassion for what happened." Must I really spell out everything for her? "I will say again, though, that I am sorry. I'm sorry I did that, with the letter. I'm sorry to you, and to Mom and Dad." And, truly, I am. I believe everything Gen is telling me about myself. I've been following the story, and while I could never villainize my own living self, I can still see how everything that happened had an effect on my parents and Gen, just as it must have done on me.

Gen seems satisfied enough with my response to move the conversation on. That, or she's given up trying to understand. "In any case, however screwed up that art trip was, it wouldn't have happened if it weren't for me."

"How do you figure that?"

"I'm the one who blabbed to our parents about you giving your spot to Ryan in the art show. I should have just left it." Gen crosses her legs, drums her fingers on the side of the mug. "You never trusted me after that. You were so mad that I had told them. Said I was just like them, assuming that you weren't capable of handling things. But what was I supposed to do! You were cutting it really close. They had their flights booked and everything. I just felt like you were burying your head in the sand every time I asked you about telling them. You did that a lot when we were growing up."

"I know. I even remember how much it drove you crazy."

Gen looks at me across the table. "Why were you like that? Why did you always act so passive and indifferent? One minute you'd be so joyful and engaged with me, and the next you'd be walking away wanting to be alone."

I shift in my seat. "It wasn't that I was indifferent toward you. I would just shut down. I didn't exactly love getting bossed around all the time."

Gen averts her eyes.

"The same way I'm sure you hated it when Peter told you to do this or that," I continue. "But I didn't *have* anyone small to boss around. You know, they always say it's the middle child who has the most issues. 'Middle child syndrome' and all that. But I'm not so sure." I say all of this in as conversational a tone as I can muster, because I don't want her to think I'm bothered by it. Because, truly, I'm not. It's all in the past, and what difference does it make now? Older or not, she's my sister. Perhaps there was a power dynamic when we were younger, but she was just a kid doing what older sisters do. Besides, I remember how annoying I could be. I'm sure I would have done the same things to me as well. "Speaking of Peter, how is he?"

Gen shrugs. "He's good. Still the golden child who can do no wrong. He has a full-time career with the fire department in Hamilton and started seeing someone really lovely. Unlike me, he has his life on track and is doing what he always wanted to do."

"Fight fires."

Gen nods. "Fight fires."

I suddenly remember the small fire we had in the first house that I can recall living in. A timber-frame bungalow with a sketchy potbelly furnace. Too small for all five of us really, but it was all our parents could afford to rent at the time. I must have been about three. It's one of my earliest memories. Us, the kids, stuffed into the station wagon parked safely afar, watching through the window as the fire engines pulled up. Peter was enthralled by the excitement, his face pressed to the window. I don't even remember the fire itself, only that it was more of a smouldering mess in the furnace that left black marks up the living room walls. Luckily, nothing burnt down, but we had to live in a hotel for a while.

"I'm glad he's happy," I say.

"Me too." Gen finishes her latte and starts to put on her coat. "Come on. All this talk about Ryan's stupid letter reminded me of something I want to show you."

"Okay, where we going?" I say with a smile and float to standing position.

"Home."

* * *

Genevieve knew it would be difficult to read the letter again, but she felt compelled to. At the back of her closet in a box on the floor, she dug around for an envelope full of cards – Christmas cards, birthday cards, thank you cards and the like. Ghost Claire hovered behind, watching intently.

Finally, Genevieve found the fat yellow envelope and pulled it out. It was stuffed with cards, but it wasn't difficult to find the one she was after; it was the largest card, both in height and width. The card was made of thick, creamy cardstock with mint green and silver foil designs all over it. *On your birthday, Sister* was scrawled across the top in metallic, shiny print. It even had little silver bows attached to the front, and when it opened, it folded out like an accordion in three sections. Inside beneath the printed "Happy Birthday" note, Claire had written: *See you at Thanksgiving! Miss you. Love, Claire.* Tucked into the card was also a single sheet of lined paper folded in half. On one side of the paper was a handwritten letter from Claire to Genevieve on her 23rd birthday, dated August 4, 2017.

–You sent this to me the summer before you met Ryan. It's the last thing you ever gave me.

The year after that, the dissolution of Claire's interest in her family was already well underway, and for Genevieve's birthday in 2018, Claire only sent a quick text. At least it was something; by that point, Claire was arguing with their parents about starting her fourth year, and Genevieve was the last family member Claire was still somewhat conversing with. But it would only be two months later, shortly before Thanksgiving, that

Genevieve would never hear directly from Claire again.

Genevieve brought out the letter and sat on her bed to read it aloud. Claire's swirly cursive font stared back up at her, slightly slanted to the left. Was it really *her* sister's writing? Her sister's words? It was so hard to swallow. It felt like an entirely different person wrote that letter. In the past, Claire usually sent some sort of miniature painting to Genevieve for her birthday, so it had been a nice surprise when Genevieve opened the card to find a letter inside instead. Claire wasn't much of a communicator via written word, and what she did write she kept for her journals. Perhaps for that reason it had felt extra special to receive the letter that year, especially since Genevieve had graduated earlier that spring and was having a really tough time finding any consistent work. Claire knew all about it and had been a great comfort, validating Genevieve any time she called to rant about getting a rejection email or no word back after an interview. Even though that summer and fall had been painful and bleak for Genevieve, and she felt like a total failure after graduation, Genevieve wished she could go back to that summer, to the day when she received that birthday letter. She would have opened it slowly and cherished reading it for longer. And she would have called her sister right away to say thank you instead of waiting a few days because she was feeling sorry for herself and couldn't muster the energy to talk to anyone.

She began reading the letter to ghost Claire:

Dear Gen,

Happy birthday! I cannot believe you're already 23. Time flies when you're old heheh.

I'm sure you'll find this far too sentimental and probably cringe your little goth heart out, buuuut one of us has to say it. Honestly, you are simply the bestest sister a girl could ask for. Of course, we've had our disagreements, we've fought like the dickens before, and yet at the end of the day, you've always been there for me. I've found that friends come and go, but you are my <u>best</u> friend, as well as my sister, and I know we have something that no one else does.

Did you knoooow thaaaat – you're actually the only person in the whole world I am always at ease with? Nowww you knowwww! We can be serious, girly, or crazy, we can still play Barbies, we can still pretend we're having high tea with the queen, and it always feels right. So I want to thank you for that; the specialness of what we have will never die.

And I know this year has been difficult for you with trying to find a job and such. But don't give up. If there's anyone who will prevail and get what they want, it's you. I should know from all the bossing around you did as a kid! Jk.

But for real, though, you'll figure it out. You always do. Just don't forget to bee bop n' boo beep n' lippity schmipity doo. Mmm'kay?

I love you, big sis! And no matter how often I tell you to "Get stuffed mate", I always will.

Happy birthday!
Love always,
Claire
Xoxoxo

PS. O yonder there, ye better hath a cocktail on me — don't make me get the hose!

No matter how many times she read it, she always cried. All their dumb inside jokes, all the nuances of her sister's cursive, the tone of the letter so emblematic of Claire...her little sister was in there, in those words. How could the same person who wrote them now hate her? Every time she read it, she was reminded how much she'd failed as a sister. Because that must be the only possible answer. Claire must have been wrong when she'd written that letter. They clearly *didn't* have a special bond. Genevieve clearly *wasn't* the best sister ever. Claire was either wrong and the letter wasn't true to begin with, or if it had been true, at some point Genevieve had ruined things. She was the older one. She ought to know better. That's what her parents had always said any time one of them caught both sisters doing something bad. Claire they could understand; she was the baby. *But you, Genevieve, you're the big sister. You ought to know better.*

Part of the surprise of receiving the letter was that Genevieve hadn't realized that that was how her sister felt about her. Perhaps on the surface, yes, she'd known. They got along well enough. But deep down? Genevieve hadn't *really* known. Claire was always so difficult to connect with because when she'd had enough, that was it. She'd disappear into her paintings or her journal. Especially when Claire went to a different high school – that was when their split really began, Genevieve guessed. They would come home at nearly the same time but on different buses, and Claire would have stories of all her art friends that Genevieve couldn't put a face to. She didn't really know the layout of Claire's school, so she couldn't envision where any of these stories took place. And she didn't know the teachers either, so she never really "got" the funny stories about the teachers' connections with the students. Claire's life was so foreign. Even more so when Claire moved away for college. So when that letter arrived from Claire, announcing how amazing a sister Genevieve was and how they'd always have a special bond, it was a surprise, and Genevieve didn't know what to feel. What does one do with that sort of information? She'd felt awkward almost, like maybe she'd opened someone else's mail. She wished she'd honoured it more, taken it more seriously, accepted it openly and not questioned it. Because now it felt like it was a test that she'd failed. A test that was asking, *Can you be this for me? Can you truly be my sister forever?* Genevieve felt like she had pondered the question too much, waited too long to answer, and when she finally did, it had been a pitiful, uncertain "Yes". The letter was an out-of-the-blue gesture of sisterhood that she hadn't returned with much of anything. She felt guilty about that. If only she had shut her mouth the following year at Thanksgiving. If only she hadn't dismissed Claire's feelings so much. Maybe she'd still be talking to her.

If only.

* * *

My sister reads the letter slowly. It's moving to watch because I can tell she's trying not to cry at first. Her voice catches and wavers, her face reddens, and then her eyes fill with salt water so much that I imagine she can hardly see the words, and a single blink sends tears, which she wipes away, spilling down her cheeks. I can feel her heart energy emptying as she reads. Or maybe it's my own. The letter sounds like how I used to write in my journals: personable and genuine.

Suddenly, my vision of my sister sitting on her bed in the fall light of her room dissipates, and I can see my left hand writing the letter. I'm holding a generic blue pen, sitting at a desk in front of a window. It's sunny out, and as I write, Genevieve's voice reads the words from somewhere far off. There's a knowing within me that I'm in my room in a house that I share with other roommates, located near the campus. I know that I just walked home about 10 minutes ago and started writing this letter. I already have a stamp on the envelope and will drop it off at the postbox on my way back to classes this afternoon. As I write, I'm thinking of Genevieve, how special it is to have her in my life. I know I have other friends now, best friends some of them. Arguably, people who I have more in common with now than I do with Genevieve, but Gen's Gen – the person I shared a room with for more than half my life. The person who understands my imagination and with whom I can be a total derp and she'll always find it hilarious. The person who I can get angry at, furious even, and know that she will still be there the next day. I know she'll think the letter's sappy, so I put that in because even though she'll like the letter, I know she won't say it. Or won't know how to. She always thinks she's cooler than she actually is. I sign off on it, fold up the paper, put it inside the humongous card I bought, slip it in the envelope and seal it.

My vision narrows until I'm back in Gen's room, and I'm struck by this knowing I just experienced. And the fact that it's not just a knowing.

It's a memory.

Gen's still sitting on the bed, fully crying now. The letter in one hand, her face in her other, rubbing her eye. All I can do is look at her. I can't even give her a hug or hand her a tissue. And it's not dark out, so my newfound skills of turning on lights wouldn't exactly be helpful. I just float, stunned and experiencing too many feelings all at once.

"You wrote that," she says, her voice heavy. "But it's like it doesn't even matter now. I knew it was too good to be true the first time I got it. Because a year later, you…deleted me."

It feels like a dream, writing that letter, but the memory is real. I truly meant what I said in it. It's astounding to think how fast things can change within a year between you and someone you love. Going from that letter to leaving my family altogether…all I can think is that I must have really been hurting, to act so out of character.

"I remember writing it," I say.

Gen sniffles, wipes her eyes. "But I thought you had no recent memories."

"I don't," I reply. "I mean, I didn't until just now. But I remember the day I wrote the letter. It was summer of course, but I was taking a summer class, so I was actually on campus for your birthday that year. You were here, looking for a job. I remember thinking it'd be nice to send you a letter this time. It felt more right than just doing a painting again."

The whole episode of the letter – conceiving it, writing it, sending it – all of it floods back to me. I even remember the FaceTime call I had with Gen a few days after she received it. She was awkward about it, as predicted, but I knew it had meant a lot to her.

I float over to the window and give a big sigh. I'm so

happy I can remember something from my college years. I wonder what that means. Maybe other memories can be triggered too. Or maybe this was just a special, one-time thing. The bliss feeling is bubbling again, which tells me it doesn't matter. The letter was important, but it doesn't mean the same thing to me now as it does to Gen. I feel as if I already know all there is to know, but also that in time, things will surface.

I turn around and watch Gen blow her nose. She sits back against the headboard of her bed, no longer crying, but looking empty all the same.

"Thank you for reading it," I say. "It's a very special letter."

She shrugs. "It is, but it doesn't feel real anymore. The person who wrote this letter is long gone. What if I never see her again? What if the Claire I meet tomorrow is someone who doesn't remember writing it, or worse, regrets writing it?"

I float over to the bed and sit on the edge. "The person who wrote that letter isn't gone," I say. "She's right here in front of you. And if I'm what's left of living Claire, then that means I'm still inside her somewhere."

I can tell this thought makes her a bit hopeful. But that wasn't my intention. I don't want her to be hopeful about tomorrow because I have no idea what I – living

Claire – will do or say when she sees Gen. I only know that Gen has to focus on the fact that I'm here now. Something about me being here will bring her closure about tomorrow. I know this to be true. Isn't that what all ghosts are for, providing closure?

It suddenly occurs to me that maybe I'm here for my *own* closure. That would be interesting. Closure about what, though? Somehow, the falling out between me and my family doesn't seem like the answer. I wonder if it has something to do with my assumed death. I don't want to think about that right now.

"It does seem logical," Gen finally says.

I give a little laugh. "Nothing about any of this is logical."

Gen half-smiles. "Yeah, that's true." She folds up the letter and sighs. "Hopefully all shall be revealed tomorrow."

"Yeah, hopefully," I reply. But secretly, I wish today would never end.

* * *

Genevieve didn't feel like staying in the apartment any longer; she was too antsy about Sunday, and after having cried about the letter, she felt refreshed. Restless. She put her coat back on. Claire followed her out the door and asked again where they were going. Genevieve didn't really know. She just knew she wanted to be moving outside somewhere. So the two sisters simply went for a walk, and Genevieve continued the story about what happened after the art show. She felt safer now with ghost Claire, not that she'd felt threatened before exactly. But since Claire's apology in the café and the birthday letter and getting through the worst of the art show story, Genevieve could see that ghost Claire wasn't exactly like the Claire she'd grown up with. She'd been worried that the ghost before her would start to shut down and retreat the more Genevieve revealed. That's what Claire had often done growing up. Genevieve had been worried the ghost would become upset or embarrassed by her actions, or that she would start to remember why she disliked her family, and Genevieve would be rejected all over again. But none of those things were true. Ghost Claire was somehow an evolved iteration of Claire. All the distilled, pure-hearted elements that had probably always been in her now manifested as this wise, acceptive entity. Genevieve trusted her implicitly.

Which was a far cry from where things had been following the art show. The relationship between Claire and her parents was strained that entire summer. Neither party could fully trust the other.

As the two sisters moved along a quiet residential side street, Genevieve explained to the ghost that there was a discussion resembling a truce, with a lot of conditions attached to it. Claire laid out several terms – her parents had to apologize to Ryan over FaceTime, they weren't allowed to talk about certain subjects with him, they were to be nicer when asking him questions, and they had to drop the edge of prejudice they seemed to carry towards him and his life decisions. Because of the sensitive situation, their parents felt they could do nothing except agree.

Meanwhile, Claire still talked to Genevieve occasionally as the summer went on, once she had forgiven Gen for prematurely telling their parents about the art show. Genevieve told Claire she'd clearly been procrastinating by not telling their parents about giving her spot away to Ryan. *I know you*, Genevieve had said. *You would've left it way too late.* Claire retorted that Genevieve had it all wrong. She said she was biding her time, waiting for the right moment, but then Genevieve had ruined it by impulsively blurting out the truth. *It made me look bad.* That, in Genevieve's opinion, was something Claire had managed entirely on her own, but she held her tongue at that point, tired of the back-and-forth.

Even though the girls still talked that summer, it was not the same. Ryan usually hovered in the background somewhere, and, like her parents, Genevieve felt she had to walk on eggshells in terms of what she said and didn't say, even though Claire hadn't given her any "terms" like she had to their parents. The thing that made it all the more difficult was the fact that Claire was so far away. It wasn't like she was just around the corner on campus and Genevieve could pop over and tell her to her face how ridiculous she was being. Maybe it was for the best, though, because if they had lived close by, Genevieve's dad could not guarantee that he wouldn't punch Ryan in the face if he ever saw him. To him, Ryan was the perpetrator in all of it. He could not believe that his own daughter would act that way without being under the duress of someone else.

But Genevieve was inclined to think that it wasn't entirely Ryan's fault, or perhaps not even his fault at all. Maybe it was all Claire's. Because regardless of how Ryan acted or what he said, Claire was the one allowing it all to happen, allowing him to speak that way about her parents, allowing him to impose conditions and insist on apologies without offering anything in return. Claire was allowing for the great divide. And perhaps she wanted it.

But even as Genevieve said that to her parents, she wasn't entirely sure that was true either. She could never forget what she'd read in Claire's journal about what Ryan had said, like he was poisoning Claire's mind. Was it intentional? Was he really trying to control and manipulate her? Or was Claire just weak minded for believing in him so zealously? Genevieve couldn't say for sure, and she had never discussed the journal with anyone.

Towards the end of that summer came the issue of paying for Claire's fourth year. Their parents had always agreed to pay for each of the kids' schooling as needed; they didn't want them to be burdened with huge debt after graduation. *There'll be plenty of opportunity for that later,* Genevieve's dad always said. They'd put Peter through school, though part of it had been paid for with a scholarship from his outstanding academic performance. They'd put Genevieve through school – no scholarships there, not that they'd been expecting any; her grades had always been so-so. But she'd agreed to work part-time and pay for her own rent, food and utilities during school with no allowance from her parents, except holiday and birthday money.

Then came Claire, who had shown artistic promise in high school. Artistic excellence. Artistic achievement.

She was a rising star. The big anticipation was that she would get a free ride through college. Scholarships galore. But she didn't get a single one. Genevieve never understood why.

Their parents tried to hide their disappointment, but it was obvious they'd been counting on the scholarships because they both had to scramble to bring the funds together for Claire's first year of school, after having gone through their divorce the year before. It was a miserable time, and although they insisted to Claire that it was totally okay, as they'd agreed to financially support each child long ago, the whole situation had an edge to it. They blamed each other for not being financially prepared for Claire's schooling. *You shouldn't have bought that motorcycle. Well,* you *didn't need to go on that wine tasting tour last year, but there we are.*

Genevieve remembered when Claire said to her how much she hated being at home that summer. She always felt like she was meant to be the bright light in their parents' lives at that time because of the divorce, and this was just another let-down. Claire felt like a failure after not getting the scholarships. It made her rethink getting a fine arts degree altogether. Maybe she should just paint as a hobby. Maybe she should try out some other electives first, to see what interested her. Genevieve talked her out of it, saying this was what she'd always wanted, wasn't it? For as long as Genevieve could remember, Claire loved art and dreamed about owning an art gallery, putting on exhibitions, exhibiting her own work around the country, selling paintings to international buyers, and running painting workshops out of a nifty warehouse studio. Most parents would say that having a fine arts degree would never lead to a "real job." But Genevieve's parents encouraged Claire because they believed she might be the next van Gogh. It was a lot of pressure, sure, but their encouragement allowed Claire to do what she really wanted. After the news about the scholarship, though, and the disappointment on their faces, Genevieve remembered Claire saying to her how she had a suspicion that they wanted to see a return on their investment in her. *We'll fork out the money if you promise to become a famous artist.* Of course, their parents had never actually said that to Claire, but Claire said that's how it kind of felt, going into college.

Genevieve dismissed it at the time because it was ludicrous. Didn't Claire know their parents at all? They would never think that way about their own kids; they were too wrapped up in their own misery to think up something as heartless as that. But then, after everything that happened with the art show, Genevieve wondered if maybe it was true, even subconsciously. What if they *did* want to see a return on their investment in Claire's fine arts degree? What if they *did* have an underlying desire for Claire to prove herself to them more than her siblings ever had to? Then again, that poisoned thinking was something that could have easily been placed in Claire's mind by Ryan. God only knows what else he'd said to her during their initial months together. He may have told Claire exactly what she wanted to hear about more things than one.

Genevieve knew without a doubt that her parents were generous and protective souls. They were not the most emotionally developed, that much had always been clear, but when it came to their offspring, they had always given them what they wanted. So, ultimately, they agreed to pay for Claire's fourth year, despite her rude behaviour towards them the past several months. But they had conditions of their own. They wanted Claire to promise that her grades and classes would come above all else, especially boyfriends, and she was absolutely not to pass up any sort of opportunity to further her career without first discussing it with her parents. And at the end of the school year, she had better secure a place in the art show. *So, get painting.*

It was then that Genevieve temporarily moved back

to her childhood home where her mother still lived, so that Genevieve could work a crappy part-time job at the Starbucks in town. It had been over a year since she'd graduated, and she was grumpy and feeling unsuccessful, unable to find a proper job still (or one that she actually cared about). She didn't even like her degree that much and ultimately felt lost and dumb. She was losing patience with Claire's angst by the day. Every time they talked, Claire was largely disinterested in Genevieve's problems, and Genevieve was bored hearing about how ridiculous Claire thought their parents' conditions were. *It's so controlling. I'm not a child.* Genevieve wanted to tell her how silly she was being, and that she actually agreed with what their parents had instructed Claire to do. But she couldn't quite say it, so she'd just breeze past it and ask about other things that didn't really matter. By that point, Claire had stopped genuinely laughing at their inside jokes, and Genevieve never asked after Ryan, which deeply bothered Claire. Both girls seemed to be growing up while outgrowing each other, and deep down, Genevieve had a feeling that wasn't how things were supposed to be between them. It wasn't their natural modus operandi, but then again, it was an abnormal time for them. Unfamiliar territory. It was natural for relationships to change as people evolved, but with Claire it felt like something was being destroyed, and Genevieve couldn't quite put her finger on it, or get back control of it. All of their past fights told her the issue would work itself out like it always did. Time was all they needed. Whenever they'd gotten mad at each other as kids, all they had to do was wait a few days before one of them would stroll up to the other and say, *Let's watch a movie. Let's play Barbies. Let's beat up Peter.* Anger forgotten.

Genevieve trusted that something similar would happen to them as Claire began her fourth year, but it never did. By that point, Claire had virtually stopped talking to their parents; she hadn't cut them off yet, but she didn't FaceTime them at all anymore like she used to. The thought of doing it made her anxious. Genevieve was the only one she still regularly spoke to.

By the time Thanksgiving rolled around, Genevieve was sick of Claire's complaining and moodiness. She had her own self-pitying problems to deal with. She had sent that message to Claire in the heat of the moment, the heat of a fight, just like they'd done hundreds of times growing up. *Why can't you just come home for Thanksgiving? It's really not a big deal. Grow up.* She wanted her sister to come home because she wanted to actually see her, but it came out all wrong. She expected some sort of snotty retort, likely peppered with swear words and a personal jab of some sort. She expected to fire one right back and then for things to be silent for a while. She expected Claire probably wouldn't come home for Thanksgiving after all that, but that they'd start to talk again afterwards. Genevieve did not expect to be ghosted. She felt as if she'd been lured into an unfair game. A game which she'd played before, but the rules had now changed without anyone telling her. She felt like her sister should have warned her beforehand, told her how hurt she really was about their parents, how sensitive things really were in her world. Genevieve didn't realize how precarious her relationship with Claire was; it seemed much of it had already eroded for Claire, enough for her to feel that blocking her own sister was justified in that moment.

But maybe Claire *had* told her, and Genevieve just hadn't listened. Maybe the signs had been there all along. Maybe the split had begun the moment Claire stepped on a plane that was headed for a school three time zones away. Or perhaps it had started the instant Claire stepped onto a different bus for her first day of high school. Maybe it had even started eroding the day Genevieve moved out of her shared room with Claire and down the hall into Peter's old room once he left for college. Or perhaps they'd begun drifting apart the night Claire put the torn-up note in Genevieve's bed. What if Claire had been aware of all of this, and Genevieve was the oblivious one?

Immediately after blocking her sister, Claire blocked her parents and brother, too. Then the next day, she dropped out of school.

* * *

The more Genevieve tells me about me, the more I start to disassociate. I feel I've been split – no, cloned. And my clone has turned evil, and I'm the good one. Yet, at the same time, we're the same person. How can that be? It's paradoxical. I've always loved a good paradox, but not this one.

Actually, I can't truly say that living Claire turned evil; I feel that she was more so misguided. No, that's not the right word either. Who am I kidding? I can't say a bad thing about myself. I know I must have done what I did for a reason that seemed really good to me at the time. A reason that I felt no one else understood except this Ryan fellow. Something deep and painful. It couldn't have come from out of nowhere. It couldn't have manifested simply because of Ryan. I knew I could be stubborn, but would I really have let a guy affect me like that?

I try to conjure up any negative feelings I might have had growing up. Misdirected anger, long-held grudges, jealousy, loneliness, feeling unloved, feeling like the odd one out, feeling like a burden. These all seem like things I might have experienced, but it's just no good; as a ghost, I can't access those darker memories and thoughts. Not willingly, at least. My essence is only drawn to warmth and laughter and goodness. The bliss strums my soul.

Gen wants to walk and walk, so I float and float. Weaving in and out of strangers, following my sister around, just like Sparky did. I dare say I feel as joyful as that loveable dog. Oh, I wonder if I'll see him now that I'm a ghost. And Jezebel too. The thought makes me want to give Gen a huge hug. I reach out a hand, and unbeknownst to her, it moves right through the cascades of her hair.

"After that," she says, "our parents were furious."

I move around to face Gen, drifting backwards as she walks forward. "What did they do?"

"They couldn't get the tuition money back, so not only was it an emotional hit but a financial one too. Not that it really matters, but you can imagine how they felt about all their hard work gone to waste."

"How do you think Claire felt?"

Gen looks caught off guard. She stuffs her hands in her pockets further. "I don't know. She probably felt…smug. Happy. I don't know."

It's a lazy answer. She should know better. "Come on, now. How do you *really* think I'd be feeling if I gave up my passion *and* cut off my family all in the span of a few days?"

I can tell she's bothered by my line of questioning. She doesn't want to consider it. Has probably avoided considering it before now.

My sister turns a corner and shrugs her shoulders. "I guess it would have been shitty. Conflicting. Maybe scary." She pauses as she walks along. "It's a hard thing to come back from. You'd have to be pretty convinced it was what you really wanted."

"What do *you* want?"

We pause at the light, wait for it to tell us to cross. Finally, the light changes, and as we start moving, Gen sighs and says, "I want things to go back to the way they were. I want for none of this to have ever happened. The stuff with Ryan, the art show, all of it. I want to rewind time."

That wasn't exactly what I had in mind, so I rephrase the question. "Okay, what is something you want that you could actually have?"

Gen's shoulders sag as she slows to a halt, considering my words. We've stopped in front of an antique shop. Together, we stare at the old furniture and trinkets through the glass. Then Gen turns to me, her eyes watery. "You're right," she says. "Nothing will ever be the same again between us. We can never go back. Even if things go well tomorrow."

"Forget about me. Forget about tomorrow," I say. She's still not getting it. "What do you want in life right now? Where do you want to be?"

Gen stares at something in the window. Either the vintage doll set or the miniature rocking chair, I can't tell. I notice there's only her reflection in the glass. I'm nowhere to be found.

"Honestly," she says, "I want to quit the daycare. And I don't want to work in marketing. I couldn't care less about it. I only took that degree because I thought I was doing the right thing."

"Ha. But the right thing, whatever that even means, is not always the best thing."

"Why do I get the feeling you're wiser as a ghost?"

"Because I am."

Gen gives a half smile. "Well, you're right. Marketing and the daycare *aren't* the best thing for me anymore.

What I'd really like to do is...travel." She seems surprised by her own answer. I'm not that surprised. She was always a dynamic individual.

"What's stopping you? You said you had some funds saved up."

Gen shrugs. "I dunno. I feel like I've been waiting, living in a haze the last few years. Here, but not really. Assuming things will...change on their own. Get better. I don't know."

"Waiting for what exactly?"

"You, I think."

Again, she seems surprised by her own answer. But once again, I'm not.

* * *

How does someone ever really know the reality of someone else? It was a question Genevieve thought a lot about after her sister disowned them. When Claire dropped out of school, Genevieve could not understand how her little sister, who had been obsessed with painting and art since she could hold a brush, would willingly drop out of a prepaid art education. She'd been so close to finishing, to getting her degree. Why end it?

No matter what reasoning Genevieve tried to come

up with, it didn't matter, because unless she could see the world through Claire's eyes, she would never really know. It seemed to her that Claire had built up some sort of false reality that supported the decision to leave her passion behind. Either that, or Claire had outgrown her passion and had been trying to tell her family for ages. Maybe that's why she hadn't given Genevieve a painting for her 23rd birthday. What if she was sick of doing them? Genevieve could never imagine her sister getting sick of making art. It was all she'd wanted growing up. If it was built into her soul, how could she have abandoned it?

Without really thinking, Genevieve led them to the local rec centre, which had an outdoor rink. It wasn't cold enough yet to ice the rink, so a group of boys were playing hockey on roller blades. Genevieve made her way to a set of empty bleachers to sit and watch.

Ghost Claire spent a few moments floating through all the bleachers as fast as she could, a big grin on her face. Then she went out into the rink and pretended to play hockey with the boys by following them around, trying to kick the small ball they were using as a puck. They of course had no clue she was there. Genevieve chuckled at the silly faces Claire made at them.

Suddenly, though, Claire's foot made a connection

with the ball and sent it flying across the rink. The boy who had been chasing it was startled and nearly tripped. Genevieve gasped. How was that possible? Ghost Claire was transparent, immaterial, metaphysical. And yet, in the span of two days, she'd figured out how to turn lights on and off, and now she was kicking pseudo-pucks around. Genevieve wondered if ghost Claire would become more stable in this realm, more tethered; perhaps she'd morph into the "real world" and swap places with the living, breathing Claire. Then Genevieve would have her sister back. What a thing to fantasize about. The longer ghost Claire was here, the less Genevieve understood about the mechanics of ghosthood.

Genevieve watched as her sister haunted the rink some more. She remembered how much her sister loved wintertime because of the snow. Claire's favourite holiday song to sing was *I'm Dreaming Of a White Christmas*, and as soon as the first snow fell in early December, she was always the first one to notice. She'd drag Peter and Genevieve outside to go sledding or have snowball fights. Genevieve didn't mind the winter, but she didn't love it like Claire did. Christmas had always been Claire's favourite holiday, while Genevieve preferred Halloween. Pretending to be someone else for a night had its appeal.

She started thinking about what Claire had asked earlier, about what Genevieve wanted out of life. Once Claire had posed the question, the answer seemed so obvious; Genevieve wanted very little of what her current life was. She didn't want to work in the daycare. Didn't want anything to do with marketing. Perhaps she didn't even want to be in this city anymore. She'd kept within driving range of her parents so that she could keep an eye on them and know that, at any moment, she could visit her childhood home, but why did she need to keep doing that?

The last five years since Claire left just felt like a fog. A fog of waiting. And shrinking. Genevieve didn't feel like she'd achieved much of anything. Drifting from entry-level job to entry-level job to part-time gigs to being on E.I. for a few months. Watching friends get married and start families while she still dated around noncommittally. Not that she *had* to start a family herself. But at least they were doing something. Her 30s were fast approaching, and all she wanted was for things to go back to before. Before Claire left them, before Claire met Ryan, before Genevieve went away to college. She wanted to begin again, pick a different degree, pick a better job, do things right by Claire, be a better sister from the start.

She'd always felt that, unlike Claire, she was not a creative person. Genevieve wasn't really sure what her hobbies were. Outside of work, she liked to read and go for walks. She liked to do puzzles while watching sitcoms. She wasn't a fan of cooking but enjoyed making desserts sometimes, mostly Halloween-themed baking. She loved learning about history and other cultures and loved to drive. But none of that amounted to a sure direction in life.

She thought she had changed a lot in the past five years, but maybe she hadn't. Perhaps it was only Claire who had evolved. She'd at least traveled to a school in a whole new part of the country, while Genevieve stayed close to home. Even though Ryan had been problematic, Genevieve saw from his social media accounts that he and Claire had stayed together the whole five years, and they looked genuinely happy in the posts he shared. Pictures of them together on a beach, a hiking trail, a bus. Photos of Claire grinning at the camera. Photos of them dancing. Photos of them at the farmer's market. Of course, anything could be going on behind the camera, but at face value, they really did seem to be in a solid, long-term relationship. And even though she'd dropped out, Claire's passion for painting was something she'd started as a little kid and continued right into school. And who knew what Claire did for a living now? Ryan's social media feed never seemed to give that away. For all Genevieve knew, Claire might well be a stay-at-home mom behind the scenes. She felt so far removed from the sister she'd grown up with, this person whose DNA she shared. She couldn't even be sure if her sister still took milk and sugar in her tea, or drank it at all anymore.

The tea. It was one of the last thoughts she'd had by herself before ghost Claire appeared. Had that only been two days ago?

Whatever the truth was about Claire's current lifestyle, it seemed to Genevieve that Claire had lived a fuller life than her by now, even while disowning her nuclear family.

Ghost Claire finally left the boys alone and made her way up to Genevieve, who tried to remember the very last time she saw her sister, the living one. In person, it had been the spring break trip. Over video call, it would have been sometime during the summer right before the Thanksgiving that ended it all. However, that was not the last time Genevieve ever heard from Claire again. She'd been saying that it was, but technically it wasn't.

Throughout the past five years, everyone had tried to reach Claire at least a few times, but to no avail. Early on,

Genevieve's mom had tried to circumvent this by directly contacting Ryan's parents, hoping to appeal to them, parent to parent. None of the Fowler family had met his parents or even spoken to them; they had never gotten the chance. And it was only Genevieve and her mother who had actually ever met Ryan himself in person.

Genevieve's mother found Mrs. Matar online one day and messaged her. The reply she got back was a shock. *Who do you think you are? I don't know you. And from what I've heard, I don't want to.* Genevieve's mother never responded. She just cried and cried. What had this Ryan fellow been telling his parents about his new girlfriend's family? It had infuriated Genevieve so much that she'd been tempted to send her own message to Mrs. Matar to tell her how messed up her son was, but she couldn't do it. She simply didn't have all the facts yet. She couldn't figure out how much of all this was Ryan's fault or Claire's. Or her own family's. Had Claire been brainwashed by these people? Or had they been the perfect catalyst to finish something that started a long time ago?

Later on, Genevieve's mother tried a different tactic; she emailed Ryan directly. She asked him to pass on a message to Claire. She wanted her to know that they would still be there for her, and that she and Claire's father just wanted to talk to her directly, in person, to figure this all out. In the message, she tried to appeal to Ryan's empathy by asking him how did he think *his* parents would feel if he ever disowned them? She said to Genevieve later that day in the garden how ridiculous it was that in order to have a personal conversation with her own daughter, she had to go through the very person whom she believed was the perpetrator of it all.

Everyone had their theories about what the problem was; Genevieve's mother had been saying from the beginning that all of this was entirely Ryan's doing. He was a narcissist, and he'd caught Claire in his trap. Claire had just gotten mixed up; she didn't know what she was doing, like always. It wasn't her fault she was being manipulated. Ryan was the villain. For a while, Genevieve believed it because of the timing of it all. It wasn't until just after Claire started dating Ryan that her relationship with her family began to crumble. Coincidence? Unlikely. But the more communication began to break down between Claire and her family, the less Genevieve was convinced that it was simply because of some boy and not something deeper that had been brewing well before Ryan appeared on the scene.

And Genevieve became especially less convinced

every time Ryan wrote emails back to them. His emails were entirely polite, apologetic even. He would write back that he'd passed on the message to Claire but was sorry to report that she still didn't want to talk to them. He said he'd even suggested it himself, asking Claire every now and then if she was sure she didn't want to try to make amends with her family, and she had still told him no. *And I must respect her wishes.*

Of course, he could have been making it all up, which is what Genevieve's mother thought, but Genevieve believed Ryan. She believed the tone in his emails. Her dad, on the other hand, didn't quite agree with her, nor did he agree with his ex-wife's thinking. He simply didn't know what to think anymore, and sustained his stoic act of indifference to the whole thing. Everyone made their assumptions with what little facts they had.

Things carried on like that for a while – Genevieve's mother emailing Ryan now and then to communicate something to Claire or to ask how they were, him replying back that all was well but that Claire still didn't want to talk. Genevieve's dad tending to renovations around his bungalow, pretending nothing was wrong but still getting worked up every time Genevieve's mother called him with updates about Ryan's replies. All the while, Genevieve just wanted it to end.

Then one day, Genevieve received a frantic phone call from her mother; Claire had emailed her parents directly, asking them to mail all her old paintings to her. She did not say what for. The email was short, to the point, and addressed them by their first names. She'd left them all in the closet of her childhood bedroom and had never come back to claim them, or any of her old clothes or diaries. She didn't care about those, it seemed; she just wanted the art. *What does she think she's doing, addressing us by our first names? And asking for this favour after how she's been acting? Fat chance!*

Genevieve remembered hearing her mother pour wine into a glass on the other end. Living alone in the house that she'd raised her family in, a family that was now broken, and drinking wine to ease the nerves raised by receiving an email…Genevieve felt sorry for her mother. She knew this was not what her mother had thought her life would be at this point: divorced after a long, unhappy marriage, underlying health issues coming to the surface, and now her youngest child estranged and addressing her by first name.

Genevieve had always had a longstanding desire to somehow fix both her parents' lives, to convince them that all was not lost. They could *do* something about themselves. But she wouldn't even know where a good place to start would be, so she got nowhere, ultimately. As she got older, she realized it wasn't her responsibility, but the urge to impose help on them was still there.

Her father's reaction to the request had been to write back and make Claire a deal; they would mail her artwork as soon as they'd had a proper chat, face to face, or at least on the phone or a video call. Preferably the latter. Claire wrote back and said she wasn't making deals with them. It was her right to have her own artwork sent to her.

They did not send any artwork until about two months later when Genevieve's father finally caved and sent it all carefully wrapped in a box with plenty of protection between each painting. Genevieve's mother had reluctantly agreed, but insisted that Claire e-transfer them the shipping cost – *it's the principal of the thing* – which Claire had done.

There were a handful of other instances over the years where they heard directly from Claire whenever she decided to unblock them and reply. Usually it was to tell them to stop bothering her and Ryan, and to stop using Ryan as the go-between. *It's not fair to him or to me.*

So, for a while, they did stop. All emails ceased for several months, maybe even about a year. Life went on. Genevieve got the job at the daycare. Her mother threw herself into her work at the bookkeeping office. Her father finally retired and puttered around his bungalow making pointless upgrades to it and taking up golf.

Then one day, Genevieve's grandmother was diagnosed with stage 4 cancer. Genevieve's mother's mother, their English grandmother who had looked after the girls when they arrived home early from school before Peter and before their parents. She would come round early and be there to greet them when the bus arrived. She'd make them a snack, a "pre-dinner" she'd call it, so as not to confuse them when they ate their "real" dinner later on with their parents and Peter. She'd entertain them for a while, read them a story or let them watch TV. She would only be there for about an hour and a half, as that was the gap of time that the girls would otherwise have been home alone. Then Peter would arrive from his high school bus, and their parents shortly after that from work. Sometimes Grandma would stay for dinner, but more often than not she would whisk back to her place because there was a show on TV that she liked to catch each evening, or there was something else going on in her neighbourhood that she wanted to attend. Genevieve remembered this carried on for years when she and Claire were quite little, until Genevieve was old enough to look after both herself and Claire for the short time home alone.

Their Grandma was a widow, her husband having passed away from a heart attack just before he retired. Grandma didn't love living alone, but she did like to do things in her own little way, and was quite a social butterfly, so she easily made friends left, right and centre. Every year without fail, she sent the kids a birthday card with some money in it. She was there most holidays, and had been a fond staple in Genevieve's upbringing.

When she started to wither away last winter, she lost weight and her appetite for months. She hated going to the hospital, though, and had put off getting tested, likely because she already knew the answer, until finally Genevieve's mother dragged her to an appointment in the spring. She began chemo shortly after, but the prognosis was not great.

Learning her grandmother was probably going to die within the year was a significant thing, and more than ever, Genevieve felt that surely this would bring Claire back to them, or that she'd at least get in touch with her grandmother now that this was happening; Claire had stopped speaking to her as well.

Genevieve had been hopeful when her father wrote to Claire telling her about her grandmother's diagnosis and *wouldn't it be nice for her if she could hear from you once more.* He copied Genevieve and her mother on the email as well as Ryan, in case it didn't get through to Claire's email. For good measure, her father also mentioned Ryan's uncle, who had passed away during the summer following the art show. At that time, because Claire and her parents had somewhat reconciled, they were communicating occasionally in awkward, strained ways via email and phone calls. Ryan chimed in occasionally on the email threads with his own life updates in an attempt to get to know his girlfriend's family a bit better. It was during that time that he mentioned his uncle and the cancer and then the eventual funeral. Claire's parents had consoled him as best they could, mainly in an effort to win over Claire and prove to her that they were trying.

So, in his email that spring, Genevieve's father mentioned it again, as a sort of lifeline to get through to, if not Claire, then Ryan, at least. *I'm sure, Ryan, you will be able to relate and understand, after having gone through something similar with your uncle's passing.*

But it had been the wrong move.

* * *

Genevieve is curled over her knees next to me on the bleachers. I know she's about to bring to light some fresh anguish that I inflicted in those emails about

Grandma. I remember our grandmother now. She was short with dark greying hair always pulled back into a bun, and glasses that she always left on her head except when she was reading the paper. I can't really remember anything else about our time together, just that I have an image of her in my mind, looking up at her from counter height, watching her cut up an apple for me as she smiles. Could I really have shut her out of my life too?

Genevieve tells me that my emails got colder and more distant as the years went on. She takes out her phone. "I should just find the exact email and show you," she says. "Maybe like the birthday letter, you'll regain another memory."

For some reason, I know that won't happen this time, but I don't say anything. While she's looking for the email, I ask, "And this was just earlier this year, in the spring?"

"Yes," she says. "Seems like longer, though."

She eventually pulls up an email on her phone from late April. It's from my personal address, one that I've had since I was 10. Clairedeluna88@gmail.com. Genevieve holds the phone up for me, and I decide to read the whole email chain, as it's not that long. It's just Dad's original email, then my reply back, and then Gen's final email to me. I notice Peter isn't mentioned anywhere in the thread. From what I can tell, he seems to have removed himself from this whole situation. I'm not surprised; it doesn't mean he doesn't care, but I remember he always seemed to be so far ahead of me and Gen, off doing something else we could never be a part of, because he was that much older than us.

Dad's email is what I thought it would be. It's fairly formal, but that's to be expected after the previous rocky years of communication. His email is careful, trying to convey the bad news while doing his best to get through to Claire – me. He pulls the Ryan's uncle card towards the end of the email, then signs off after typing in Grandma's full name and phone number, in hopes that I will contact her.

The next email, my response to his, is short, formal and to the point. Just as I feared, it's harsh. Cold.

Helen, Carl, and Genevieve,

I've told you countless times over the past several years to leave me and Ryan alone. Why do you still insist on contacting me? It pains me to say it, but I have no intention of contacting Grandma. And now, you've used Ryan's uncle's death as a means of guilt-tripping us into contacting her. It's not a good correlation to make, though, because unlike our family and the people in it, Ryan was actually close with his uncle.

At this point, I don't know how else to make you understand; I don't like who you are as people, and I don't love you. I have moved on from my relationship with any of you, and I suggest you all do the same.

I have no desire to hear from any of you again. Just leave me alone.

-Claire

I read it again a few times. Is this really me? Why did I do this? Reading the email doesn't pull me back into the memory of writing it, just as I predicted. It's too much negative energy. There's no way my blissful ghostliness could return there. The birthday card made sense because it was a memory full of connection and sisterhood. Positive vibes, as they say. But this...this is heartless. Could I really have been so angry to have ignored my dying grandmother? I wonder how she is now. I ask Genevieve.

"Grandma's doing okay, actually. The chemo has slowed things down, but she may not last another year, or even six months. It's hard to say." She shifts in her seat, rubbing her autumn-cold hands together. "You know how she is. Always cheery, always talkative."

I'm glad to hear she isn't gone yet.

"After we all got that email from you...well, I just about lost it. I was so mad. I don't think I've ever been madder at you. It was one thing to ignore us and be cold to us these past five years, but to do it to Grandma, who hadn't done anything wrong? And who's dying of cancer?" She shook her head. "I was finished trying to understand. I was done being nice and trying not to rock the boat."

"What did you do?" I ask.

Genevieve looks guilty. "I'm not proud of it now," she says. "It was harsh and sarcastic and childish. But you have to understand, I was *so* angry."

"I understand," I say. And I really do.

She scrolls up the email thread and lets me read the last one, from her to me, with Ryan, Mom, Dad, and now Peter cc'd too.

Claire.

I don't understand you...I have really tried, but I just can't do it anymore. It's infuriating how blind you are to the hypocrisy. You've always thought you're such a good person because you volunteered at shelters and donated art to school fundraisers. But it's clearly just *for show because then you send an email like that to your own blood relatives, one of whom is dying. Well, I don't care what reasons you <u>believe</u> that you have for justifying your actions – it's disgusting behaviour.*

You think you know us, and you think you know who I am. But you have no clue what my life has been like or what I've been doing, and that's only because YOU have chosen to not be involved. So don't you dare think you have any right to judge me or us, simply because you're the one who <u>insists</u> on living in the past. Every one of us – including you – has grown and changed over these past years. So much has changed, and yet you're the one treating this like it's a static situation.

Up until today, I willing to be open to you, despite everything. As your sister, I was willing to overlook any of your wrongdoings if you ever needed help. I was <u>still</u> open to that this whole time.

But that bridge has burned.

You are dead to me now.

From now on, I will be telling people that I only have an older brother and that I'm the youngest in my family. I'm ok with this because it's not the worst thing that could happen. Other families have actual horrific and traumatizing events occur, and you should consider yourself lucky that you've never experienced any of those things, though for some reason you believe you have.

Your loving sister who despite everything doesn't hate you but wishes you well in the afterlife,
Gen

I don't even want to finish reading it, but I do for Gen's sake. It certainly has her signature snarky tone, the same one she used whenever we fought as kids. I'm not offended by it, though. How can I be? This email was directed at a version of me that I know I – ghost me – haven't become yet. It would be like getting mad at someone who did something annoying to you in a dream you had the night before. So, no, I'm not hurt by this email. I understand why she wrote it like that. She was always one for doing things in the heat of the moment; this is clearly no different.

The problem I have with it, though, is that at the time of writing it, she still didn't get why living Claire did what she did. Gen's letter is reactionary, and she's reacting to something she had still not fully understood. That's the crux of this whole issue; no one really took the time to listen and understand. I'm starting to see the

155

divide between the sides: Claire vs. her family identity, Claire vs. Gen, Claire vs. parents. I'm starting to see the great divide because it's so obvious; neither side understands at all where the other is coming from. But Gen – Gen is the middle. She has the capacity to see both sides. She can bridge the gap, I just know it. She shares Claire's experiences growing up, and she shares her parents' experience since this whole thing started. Gen has all the answers; she just doesn't know it yet.

She's looking at me now with an uncertain expression, probably worried about what I'm going to say about her email. "Well?" she says.

"I mean, it's not great," I reply. "It's just as harsh as the one she – I – sent in the first place, if not more in some ways."

Gen slumps. "I know. I wasn't thinking. I was just...*mad.*"

"You were never good at processing your anger," I say. "You took things out on me a lot."

"I know," she says in a small voice. "I'm so sorry about that. I didn't know any better, not that that's any excuse. Mom and Dad...they made me so mad. It was like they never had real time for us." Gen wraps her coat around herself tighter, watching the skaters. "They were so consumed by their own unhappiness with each other, and so emotionally stunted in their own ways. Everything was always just swept under the rug, pushed down, pushed away. I always felt like I had to pretend things were okay. I hated doing that, whether it was repressing anger, sadness, happiness, giddiness, anxiousness, whatever."

"You were like a gushing fire hydrant," I say, my eyes also trained on the hockey players. "And I was the sponge." I imagine a big yellow, holey sponge submerged under water, or being used in a futile attempt to lap up a never-ending leak. "You know what happens when a sponge takes in too much water?" I pause for effect. "They can't take in any more. They need to be wrung out."

Gen side-eyes me. "Where are you going with this metaphor?"

I shrug. "I'm just thinking that maybe something about being with Ryan, or being at a school so far away, was my way of wringing myself out." It's strange trying to come up with reasoning for something I can't remember doing. I feel I know myself well enough, though, that I can't be too far off, right?

I turn to Gen. "Have you ever wondered why everyone is questioning *my* motivations for leaving our family? As if the fact I'm related by blood to a small group of people should be all that's needed to seal us together forever, no matter what?"

"But it is reason enough, though, isn't it?" Gen asks. "We can't change who our family members are. They are how we get our start in the world. Having a relationship with them...that's just the normal thing to do."

"There is no normal," I reply. "No one can really presume to know what normal is. But that's not my point." I shake my head and return to my original query, which she still isn't fully grasping. "People always seem to first question why a child wants to leave their family. But they should really be asking – what could possibly have happened in that family that would make a child want to leave?"

My sentiment hangs in the air between us. I feel so strongly about this angle in relation to our situation. I can't feel the cold metal bleacher beneath me, nor the bright autumn sun on my face or slight breeze in the air, but I feel this question in the depths of my soul. Like blindly reaching for keys under water and brushing up against their sharp teeth.

Gen looks out across the city like she's searching for the answer in the distance. She shrugs. "But nothing horrible ever happened in our family. Nothing weird or bad or messed up. You hear of other families going through some real tragic stuff, or something really twisted and dark, but that wasn't us. We were just a...*regular* family." She's careful to not use the word "normal."

"Everything's relative," I reply. Then I remember a line from her email. *From now on, I will be telling people that I only have an older brother and that I'm the youngest in my family.* If I had a gut, I feel this line would punch me there. Something about it now sticks out to me. I realize this is a sentiment that I've always been worried about. "When you said in your email that you'll be pretending from now on that it's just you and Peter, and that you never had a sister," I say, "I think that's already how I felt growing up."

"What do you mean?"

"It's what I always feared, that I wasn't truly wanted." Another memory pops into my third eye. Me and Gen fighting about something. There was pushing, shoving, arm scratching. I ran to Mom in the front room to complain and cry. Mom comforted me, gave me kisses on my arm and told me not to worry. *These things happen, and we always have to make up.* Then we walked around the corner, and there was Gen, sitting on the bottom steps all mopey and quiet. I could tell she'd been listening to our mother-daughter talk. Mom asked her what's wrong, and Gen said that it was clear to her that Mom liked me better, and that I was the favourite. She'd been scratched too, she said, but she figured Mom must not care as much. Suddenly, our mother left my side and rushed to comfort Gen. *Aw, sweetie*, she said. *I don't like Claire better; I love both of you equally.* For some reason that first part of her sentence always stood out to me. *I don't like Claire better.* I must have been about five or six.

"My birth was an accident," I say to Gen. "They'd planned for you and Peter. They'd wanted two kids. One of each, a boy and a girl. And they got it. Then suddenly, I came along. Unplanned. Which means unwanted, initially." Gen starts to speak but I rush on. "I know, I know. They've never acted much differently towards me than either of you. But I remember always kind of feeling tacked on to the family…like I wasn't really supposed to be there. And it wasn't until after my birth that they started to get really unhappy in their marriage. Coincidence?" I pause, shrug. "I'm sure they must have had issues before I came along, but what if having an extra kid was somehow the last straw? Suddenly, they've got this added financial strain they didn't budget for. Another baby crying. More sleepless nights. Did they resent having me? Did they take it out on each other? Their marriage really fell apart only after I came along."

For the first time since coming to this realm, I feel the hollowness of being a ghost.

"Is that really what you've thought this whole time?" Gen's looking at me, half horrified, half devastated, tears pricking her eyes.

I take in a breath. "Yes. No. I don't know!" I let the breath out, suddenly exasperated. "Sometimes, yes, I definitely remember feeling that way. It was a constant fear in the back of my head. It's not logical, I know. Of *course* they loved me. Of *course* you and Peter loved me. Of *course* I had an all-around good childhood. Logically, yes, I know that I'm wrong about being unwanted. But it didn't always *feel* that way. You can know something but not feel it."

Saying all of this out loud feels like a confession of a sin, where the sin is this horrible "what if" that I've kept hidden for so long. Even though it's not really my sin or based on truth or fact. But it doesn't matter if it's true or not; what matters is how I felt about it all while growing up.

I remember Gen would oscillate between me and Peter. One day she'd be my best friend, and we'd get on like a house on fire. Then the next, she'd be ganging up on me with Peter, joining in on his teasing about my pointed chin or stealing my paintbrushes to annoy me. It was all in good jest, all just typical sibling banter. And I know now why she did it. Just like I was her little sister, she was Peter's little sister, and she would do nearly anything to impress him, to be in his "cool" books. I know this because I would do almost anything to impress Gen. Logically, this all makes sense, the dynamic between siblings. The squabbling, the jealousy, the games, the fun. But logic doesn't matter where feelings are concerned. And more often than not, I got the feeling that I was an annoyance, a nuisance, an accident. A mistake.

It seems I've hit my own nerve. I know if I had a pulse, it would be beating like crazy. Even just thinking about all this is making my head spin. That's how I know it's real – *was* real – to me when I was alive.

I am hollow. The bliss is gone, but only temporarily. I take a deep breath in, though I can't feel any air over my tongue, and let it back out. The memory of having a body is what grounds me. I don't want Gen to worry about me; I'm just a ghost. So I do everything I can to conjure the bliss back to me.

The thoughts about feeling unwanted melt away. They don't matter to me anymore, truly they don't. But they were powerful because I know I touched on something that still matters to the living me.

Her demons are not my own, though. Not anymore. Not in this afterlife.

* * *

When Claire's ghost told Genevieve that she felt unwanted growing up, Genevieve felt like something she knew all along was being confirmed.

On the surface, it was sobering to hear her sister say those words; it didn't seem real. But deep down, she wasn't surprised at all. Deep down, she felt a horror creep up the back of her spine, a guilt-ridden horror that whispered, *You know what you did. You always knew.*

For the past five years, this fear had tugged at her, a fear that maybe she had been just a little too mean to her sister growing up. A fear that she'd sided with Peter one too many times during various fights and arguments. Genevieve was ashamed to admit to anyone just how many times she felt inclined to undermine Claire in some way, as if she had to assert power over her simply because she was the older sister. Was it because that's how Peter had treated her sometimes, and it trickled down to Claire? Or did Peter have nothing to do with it? More often than not, Genevieve had acted like she was number one, or at least "the better one," the one to be taken care of first, the one who had to be right and whose instruction should always be followed by Claire. Why had she been so competitive with Claire growing up? Genevieve wondered what she'd been afraid would happen if she wasn't always trying to come out on top. If Claire ever took the spotlight, what would that say about Genevieve?

And yet, at the same time, Genevieve would be just as likely to protect Claire and defend her, should anyone act out against her. But she couldn't really remember a lot of opportunities where that had occurred. Though they were close in age, they were far enough apart that Claire had been two grades lower than Genevieve, so they never had any elementary classes together, nor did they ever play together at recess, often sticking with their own friend groups. Then of course they went to different high schools, so there was no opportunity to stand up for Claire in that case either. Perhaps Genevieve had never really gotten a chance to act like a protective sister, and that had weakened their relationship without them knowing it. Even at home, Genevieve would either be on Claire's side already because they were playing together, or she'd be on Peter's side poking fun at Claire.

But wasn't that what siblings did? She was just a kid. She'd done what felt natural. Most of it happened without a second thought. She'd seen enough kids at the daycare now to know how they function, and most of them followed their first whims. Because they don't know any better. Don't know enough.

Genevieve didn't feel this was a good excuse, but there wasn't anything she could do. She couldn't go back in time and change her behaviour. But now, with her sister in town – perhaps tomorrow was her chance to apologize and acknowledge her sister's hurt about her place in their family.

How exactly should she bring that up, though? Wouldn't she be assuming too much? Genevieve had to remind herself that living Claire wasn't an exact replica of ghost Claire. What if living Claire had an entirely different reason as to why she disowned them? Genevieve couldn't be totally sure that anything Claire's ghost told her was relevant to living Claire's current state of mind. At the same time, though, Genevieve knew that everything the ghost said was still important. Important, but not quite *it*.

It was all so confusing, with too many variables. It made Genevieve's head ache. She shut her eyes and put her face in her palms, massaging her hairline. Regardless of what she thought, she still felt guilty. Over the past five years, things had been so up and down with Claire, and it had only added to Genevieve's mounting fear that she hadn't been nearly as good a sister as she could and should have been. She'd skirted her responsibilities as the older sister. Clearly, that must have been the case if their bond was so easy for Claire to break off.

Genevieve couldn't help it; her eyes began to water again.

—I failed you. I completely failed you as a sister, didn't I.

She couldn't even bear to look at her ghostly sister. Genevieve didn't want to be convinced otherwise or cheered up. She felt she deserved all the misery and regret she was feeling and wanted to feel it fully. She wanted to wallow and be pathetic and feel sorry for herself. She wanted to hate herself for a little while, which she was good at doing most days anyway.

—I'm sorry, but I need to be alone right now. Please don't follow me.

Genevieve got up from the bleachers without looking back and made her way down to the ground.

As she walked along the streets, she kept expecting ghost Claire to show up next to her, but it appeared her ghostly sister was respecting her wishes to be alone. Genevieve wanted to go back home and cry in private, so that's where she went. Ever since Thursday evening, she had felt so up and down about seeing Claire on

Sunday. At times, she felt for sure it was the right thing to do. And at others, she felt herself receding from the idea.

Learning about Claire's insecurities around her place in the family was a punch in the gut. Or maybe Genevieve *wanted* to be punched in the gut. But, of course, what would that solve? What was done was done. Genevieve's deep fear was confirmed; she had not been a good enough older sister. As the middle child, she was supposed to be the glue in the family, right? At least, that's how she had often felt growing up. Why had she failed?

When she reached her apartment, Genevieve had the sudden urge to talk to Peter. She wanted to feel validated, one way or the other. When she got inside, she stripped off her outerwear and called him. He answered on the second ring. It was Saturday, and he was on call that weekend, he said, for the station. But at that moment, he was working on his downstairs bathroom reno. His longtime girlfriend Samantha was out running errands.

Peter asked Genevieve if she was okay; he said she sounded different. Suddenly self-conscious, Genevieve replied quickly she was fine and just wanted to say hi, as they hadn't talked in a while.

It was then she realized that she could never really open up to him. He was her older brother, with an actual career and home improvements to worry about. They were close, but not close enough. Instead, she asked him if he ever thought about Claire. She could almost hear his shrug on the other end.

—I mean, not really, no. I'm not sure what to think anymore if I did. I'm pretty wrapped up in other things these days anyway. Why do you ask?

Genevieve shrugged back, then remembered he couldn't see her, so she told him she just wondered. She wanted to ask him more, but it didn't feel right. They talked a bit longer about his bathroom reno and how work was going, then said goodbye.

She considered calling one of her parents, but then immediately knew that would mean an hour-long commitment to talking on the phone to either one of them. She just didn't have the energy for it. If she brought up Claire, her mother would inevitably go on about how Ryan's family stole her daughter away. And her dad would inevitably go on about how angry he was and how he just didn't understand the psychology of it all. She wouldn't be able to articulate her theories to them even if they asked, because she didn't know how to explain to her parents that their third child felt like she didn't really belong in her own family. And that Genevieve, the only one really close to Claire, had failed to recognize that.

Genevieve went to her bedroom and flopped onto the bed. She rubbed her eyes again and tried to process all that had happened in the last few days: the appearance of her sister's ghost, the panic that her sister may be dead, the confusion upon realizing Claire was actually still alive. What did it all mean?

Thinking about her parents and how the whole mess with Claire got started made Genevieve want to look at all the emails that had been exchanged over the years. Genevieve still had all of them somewhere in her inbox. She grabbed her laptop from the nightstand and opened her email. She searched for Claire's address, and all the emails that had her name in them popped up. She immediately saw the most recent thread where she told Claire she was dead to her. Genevieve clicked the next email thread, which was between just her and her parents four months earlier, but it mentioned Claire, as usual. By that point, Genevieve was writing minimal responses; she was so tired of talking about Claire and theorizing what went wrong that whenever her parents sent her long emails about the situation, she only skimmed them and replied with feigned agreement and interest. She kept going, two or more years back. There were some heated exchanges between Claire and their parents, Claire asking them to mail her artwork immediately and them trying to bargain with her. *Get on FaceTime with us and talk, then we'll mail it to you.* Genevieve scrolled on.

The further back in time she went, the less harsh the emails became. It was strange seeing the last five years condensed that way in front of her; the dissolution was so very clear. Reading everything backwards was like watching a building rebuild itself in slow motion after it had been blown up.

At one point, she scrolled too far and saw some exchanges between her and Claire during the fall, before that fateful Christmas where Claire had become enamoured with Ryan. That fall, the sisters had sent some photos back and forth: Claire sharing pictures of the campus art studio and selfies of her at work, a smear of paint on the side of her jaw, and Genevieve writing back with photos of her new short haircut she'd just gotten at the time. She told Claire she couldn't wait for her to come back at Christmas so they could walk around town again like they used to. Walk by the dance studio where they'd once taken a year of tap classes with some caddy girls. Walk past Dee-Lites, the café where they used to be able to order the most amazing frittatas, but the new owners had since changed the breakfast menu. Their little hometown was always so cute at Christmastime, and Genevieve always appreciated it more when Claire was around to fuel her excitement.

Genevieve scrolled back up into the new year during late spring, after the spring break trip but before the art show. It was there that Genevieve found the first big email Claire had ever sent to her parents about the whole *situation* that was beginning to brew, with them having just learnt about Ryan taking Claire's place in the art show. Genevieve didn't recognize it. As she began to read, she remembered hardly anything from it but knew she must have read it at the time, as she was cc'd on it. This was the email that started it all. She couldn't believe she'd forgotten about it.

Dear Mom and Dad,

I've never said anything bad about my upbringing to Ryan. I know we were luckier than most kids — but you can't deny that there were lots of issues with your marriage, and all I'm saying is that it had an effect on me. Individually, you are both great parents, and I know you've always just wanted us to be successful in life, and I know that I will be. But together as parents, it was really difficult being around your anger and instability all the time. Especially *after Peter and Genevieve left, you were always on at me to be happier, "stop being so moody," and I know you did that because you were scared I'd turn out to be as unhappy as you. But to be honest, it's too much pressure when you go on about it and try to control what I should and shouldn't be doing, just because of how <u>you're</u> feeling about something.*

I'm not sure why me dating Ryan has come as such a surprise to you both after I told you about him over Christmas. I thought I had made it pretty obvious then that he was someone special to me, but I guess not. I have to admit, I find it quite hurtful after how excited he's been about coming into my life and how welcoming his parents have been to me that you both can't do the same. I don't see why you have to meet him in person to like him; it would be nice if you just trusted me when I tell you that he makes me happy. But you're so suspicious all the time of everyone else, and it's exhausting. In all honesty, if it weren't for Ryan, I don't think I'd be getting through third year very well at all. There's a lot you don't know about.

It seems you're more concerned about my career as a serious artist, possibly even more so than my health and happiness. At least, that's what it feels like at times. For the record, though, I <u>am</u> a serious artist, and I shouldn't have to prove it to anyone by going to school or becoming "famous" with my art. It's way too much *pressure. I will do what I love regardless and will always strive to be successful, but if I happen to go into some other line of work or turn my attention elsewhere, why is that so bad? If I'm being honest, my art has become a huge source of anxiety for me while doing this degree. That's made me question a lot of things about myself, and more days than not I feel lost. I tell myself constantly that I'm a failure. But Ryan has been an anchor for me during this time. If you've never met someone in your life who's been that kind of person for you, that's not my problem, and it doesn't mean it's not real for someone else, someone like me.*

The reason I gave Ryan my spot in the art show is because he wants it more than me, and I'm too anxious and stressed out to do it anyway. So he's actually doing me a huge favour by taking my spot, plus I'm happy to support him in something he loves doing. We're both an inspiration to each other, as it should be in a relationship, and I'm not going to feel bad about that. If art isn't fulfilling me anymore, then I think I should be able to find other ways to feel good about myself, and helping Ryan is one of those things. I never felt like I could tell you any of this, though, about the art show and Ryan, because I've never been able to talk to either of you about anything emotionally serious. You were constantly wrapped up in your fights all the time that whenever I did try to say anything about how I was feeling, you would always trump me with something you were dealing with, or say "Too bad, toughen up." Maybe that was _your_ generation growing up, but it's not mine. And frankly, it's just rude and disrespectful to be that dismissive of someone else.

And for the record, all of my feelings about my art and this anxiety stuff aren't just coming out of nowhere. You keep saying I'm just being influenced by my friends and by Ryan and that I'm just "following the crowd", trying to be on trend with mental health issues. But it's not true; I've been repressing things for a very long time. All the pressure growing up to monetize my art somehow and be the best constantly while also not being taken seriously when I try to talk about something emotional – I think it's all just manifested itself into this past year. Regardless, it's disappointing and painful to know that my own parents think I'm just being selfish and weak minded. All I ask is that you both be more understanding and stop being in denial of the fact that there is an actual problem here, and it has nothing to do with Ryan.

I'm at an age where I want to decide what I do in life without having to worry about your criticism. And I want to do it freely, even if it means messing up and getting it wrong. You had the freedom to do that in life, so should I. And if Ryan is a mistake, then so what? If trying new things doesn't work out, so what? I'll deal with that if and when the time comes. But you need to let it happen. Just let me make mistakes. Let me live.

I hope you can still respect my wishes to not come to the art show; I just need some space before we talk again. And please know I'm not saying any of this to make you feel bad. I just want us to begin to make things better.

Love, Claire

Genevieve's heart pounded the further she read on, and she had twisty feelings in her gut. Feelings of regret and remorse. The letter was so completely...*reasonable*. Nothing about it was harsh or nasty or untrue. It was honest, open, vulnerable, firm, but loving too. She'd even signed it with love. *Love, Claire*. None of the letters after that were signed with love again. For a while, she'd signed, *Thanks, Claire*. Then ultimately just *Claire* with a dash before it.

Genevieve was dazed. *That* was the original letter that began everything? *That* was what her parents had received? It wasn't even bad. The letter was so incredibly easy to work with. So rational yet raw. And reading it again, Genevieve could see how much of a cry for support it was. A plea to be understood one last time by the very people who brought her into this world. How had they all managed to mess up their response to that letter? It was such an easy letter to work with. A no-brainer, in Genevieve's mind. Claire clearly stated in the email, *There were lots of issues with your marriage, and all I'm saying is that it had an effect on me.* When your kid tells you that kind of thing, Genevieve had to figure that that in itself would be a big red flag about something you've done wrong. The only appropriate response she could think of would be to listen more, and listen deeply, to hear further what the child had to say. Why hadn't her parents done that? Why hadn't *she* done that? That kind of comment from your own kid doesn't just come out of nowhere.

Genevieve wiped her eyes and blew her nose. She started to feel panicky. She felt she'd stumbled onto something crucial. She wanted to scream from the rooftops to Claire – living Claire – that she understood. *I get it.* She wanted to wave a big white flag, a gesture of surrender, in Claire's direction. As she stared at the screen with the email dated May 1, 2018, she wanted to yell at it, to the person who wrote that letter all those years ago, yell back through time into the void and say, *I see you, Claire. I understand. You're right. You are valid.*

Why couldn't she have been more aware during this time about what was happening? The answer was right there all along. If only she'd looked at those emails years earlier and studied that letter. She suddenly felt she knew everything there was to know about the situation. She finally *got it*. She understood exactly what Claire was saying because she, too, could relate. They were brought up in the same house; of *course* she could relate. So why had it taken Genevieve so long to realize?

She'd been so preoccupied the last five years of her life with her failure in securing a steady job, then finally starting a career, being able to support herself, and moving into her own apartment. She'd been so distracted by boys and tumultuous relationships to really pay attention to the dissolution of her sister's tie to their family. In truth, Genevieve had always thought that eventually, some day in the future, Claire would come back to them, so she'd never been particularly worried. At first, in the early days, she'd spent a lot of time being the middleperson, trying to keep the boat steady, trying to translate between both sides. She remembered talking to Claire on FaceTime shortly after the art show. She'd tried to get some answers from Claire. Then she'd FaceTimed her parents and tried to tell them what she'd learnt. It hadn't been enough, though. Later that year, after Claire had blocked her, she was angry at first, indifferent. But then she let it go and started believing that it was fine. Stuff like that happened in families, and she couldn't imagine it lasting a lifetime. She'd chosen to believe that it was fine because Claire would surely find her way back to them someday.

But then more years passed, and Claire coming back to them still wasn't happening. Then the whole email sequence about their grandma's cancer had came to light, and that had burst Genevieve's little bubble of hope. She'd suddenly felt so angry again, and felt like a fool for having believed there was still some good left in her sister. She'd sent that harsh email in spite, and in the heat of the moment. She'd felt pretty okay about it for a while. Then she'd started to feel bad, ultimately repressing all of it. Blocking it from her mind, the whole thing. The whole situation.

Now, her somehow-not-dead sister's ghost was here in this realm, talking to her, but the pieces still weren't quite coming together. The May 1st email, though – that was a huge missing piece. And she'd had it all along.

Genevieve thought about how much she'd grown over the past year, finally moving into her own apartment, getting the full-time job at the daycare, finally taking a break from any relationships. She'd spent more time alone figuring herself out on various levels. Things still weren't perfect, but she felt more "grown up" than she ever had before. She felt she had more perspective now. Was that the reason she was only just now able to piece this together? It seemed rational.

Suddenly, Genevieve really wanted to see Claire, the ghost version. She had to tell her what she'd found. Had to see if it prompted any memories for her. Maybe this could be ghost Claire's missing piece, too.

Genevieve called out her name into the empty apartment. Once, twice. A few more times. But the ghost did not appear.

* * *

I watch my sister leave the bleachers. I've seen her cry plenty times before, but never in this way. Usually it was tears of frustration over something Peter or I had done. She would get so angry, pacing around the room trying to get us to understand something. Her face would redden, and she'd start to exaggerate her words. Then the tears would come, as would the insults telling us how stupid we were for not understanding or listening to her instructions. Peter would always make fun of her more and provoke her. I would just walk away.

But just now, her face didn't get red. She wasn't crying out of frustration. Her expression simply crumpled, and the tears that pooled in her eyes fell silently. No sobbing, yelling or insults. Just pain.

She genuinely believes she caused our rift – she and she alone. But that's not entirely true. Maybe it's not even a little bit true. Maybe neither of us caused it. Maybe it was a byproduct of something else.

My sister leaves the park, and I remain on the bleachers, unsure of what to do. The boys are still playing hockey. It occurs to me that for the first time in the past two days, I don't feel tethered to Gen as she walks away. I am my own entity. I feel the desire to make my own choices. It's disturbingly too real for a ghost. I wish I felt lighter. What's happening to me?

Finally, I begin to move and float out into the open air. I float over the city aimlessly. Everyone looks so small from up here. Then I move downward to street level and watch the people as they walk right through me. I pass by the antique storefront Gen and I stood at before. Down and around the corner a few streets over, I find a cemetery. A really old one, the oldest in the city, or so the plaque says. It's enclosed by a low stone wall, and there's a big gated archway at the front. The rows of headstones, crumbling and crooked, look like the black and grey fingertips of a giant reaching up from the ground. I wonder why I haven't seen any other ghosts, especially here of all places.

I float around the cemetery for a while and ponder my existence, trying to remember what happened the moment before I first saw Genevieve two days ago. I know there must be some reason why I'm here. Maybe I'm here only because of Genevieve. Could I be a figment of her will? An angel sent to guide her? No, that doesn't feel right. I am a ghost, through and through. Ghosts are people who were once alive. But the earthly version of me *is* still alive. How can we coexist? I wonder what will happen tomorrow when I see my living self.

It's all so confusing. Too many variables.

I'm not sure how much time has passed before I feel it. A tug right in the middle of where my heart would be if I had one. I know it's Genevieve. I need to go to her, and although I can't remember the city's layout very well, I need only follow the pull to get back to her apartment.

I haven't gone far when suddenly the tug ceases; she's stopped calling. She's given up. I pause in the middle of an intersection, unsure where to go next. The light turns green, and traffic starts to move through me. I don't even flinch.

I turn around, looking at each of the roads. I face a white SUV that's heading straight for me, and I'm suddenly overcome with déjà vu. The chipped black roof rack looks so familiar. I hear a passing pedestrian's high-pitched laugh, and out of the corner of my eye, a chocolate lab walking its owner barks – sounds that I feel like I've heard before in that very sequence. The car doesn't stop. I have the feeling it's going to hit me. Instinctively, I shield myself and give a little scream, closing my eyes. The car rushes through me, and unlike the other cars, it pulls me through the air a bit so that I stumble.

Quickly, I hover out of the road and onto the sidewalk, then into an alcove. My breath is coming quickly, and it feels like my heart is beating fast, but of course I have no such thing. Everyone carries on, completely unaware of my existence, just like that car had been.

It seems the more time passes in this realm, the more I'm having physical sensations. Turning on lights, kicking hockey pucks, and now this SUV experience. The bliss feeling is less present the more my thinking becomes concrete and less abstract. The threat of that car felt real. It even physically dragged me a little, somehow.

For the first time since becoming a ghost, I feel fear. I don't want to be tethered to this realm like this forever – here, but not really. Alive, but not really. I don't want my experiences to become more human. It doesn't seem natural for the state I'm in. Doesn't seem right. The longer I'm here, the more I feel like something is becoming set in stone. My death, probably.

My death hasn't happened yet, though. That much is clear. But the potential for it happening is becoming more of a sure thing.

And then, all at once, it descends upon me; that's why I'm here. It must be. I'm here to stop my death from happening.

I float out of the alcove and pick a direction, knowing it's the right one because it has to be. I have to find Genevieve.

* * *

The late afternoon sun sank steadily towards the skyline. Genevieve had done nothing all day except curl up on her bed and cry herself to sleep. She missed her sister, both the ghost and the living one. Claire hadn't appeared when she'd called her name. At first, Genevieve panicked, thinking that she had broken the spell and done something wrong by telling Claire not to follow her. What if Genevieve was the only thing tethering her to this world, and by sending her away, she'd erased her? After feeling anxious about that for a while, which fed more into her anxiousness to speak with Claire, she'd become exhausted and fallen asleep.

Genevieve sat up on the bed, hoping to see Claire hovering somewhere, but the room was empty. She got up, showered, and put on her pyjamas; she knew she wouldn't be going out again today.

She had the sudden urge to try Claire again. Genevieve called out softly into the empty apartment.

–Claire, are you there?

* * *

"I'm here," I say.

Gen whips around and smiles in relief. Her eyes are very puffy and red. "I'm so glad you're still here. I thought you were gone forever." She comes towards me like she's going to give me a hug, then stops.

"We need to talk." We both say it at the same time.

Although I want to share my news with her right away, I smile and say, "You go first."

We head into the living room where Gen sits on the couch with her laptop. "I found something that really put everything into perspective for me."

"What's that?" I ask.

She gives me a serious look, one that penetrates into my soul. She's not looking through me; she's looking at me. "I get it now. Everything," she says. "I understand *everything.* I know exactly why you did what you did."

I'm not as excited as she is about this revelation, but that's to be expected. It's not my thing to be excited about. It's hers. Nonetheless, I'm curious to hear what she's found out. She reads me some sort of letter that I apparently wrote at the beginning of when this all started. It's dated after the March break trip but before the art show. The letter sounds sincere, honest. I'm actually proud of myself for having put it together and standing up to our parents that way. It's not something I would normally ever do. Whenever I was feeling angry or hurt or left out about something, I would just go inward to my paintings and stay there till it passed. It seems to me that after everything Genevieve has told me, something about being with Ryan brought it out of me, this quiet fire that I'm hearing in my letter.

Gen finishes reading it, and a few moments of silence pass between us.

"What do you think?" she asks. "Did it bring back any memories for you?"

I smile. So that's why she wanted to read it to me so badly. I shake my head. "No, it didn't stir anything." I float across the room to the armchair. "But, Gen, I don't need to get my memory back in order to give you answers. You already have all the answers you need.

They've always been there."

Gen closes her laptop thoughtfully. "You know, that's actually what I was thinking earlier...how this letter has always been here, the whole time, but I didn't understand it till now. Didn't even remember it existed before today."

"So go on, then," I say. "Tell me what it means to you."

Gen puts her laptop on the coffee table and sighs, choosing her words carefully. "All you wanted was to be understood. And supported. Like fully, emotionally, unconditionally supported." Gen waves a hand. "Not academically or financially. Not materialistically. Those had always been there. Our parents have always supported us in those ways, as all parents should. But the most important thing of all was missing for you. That emotional safety, that true support and understanding. Trust. Without that, all the other types of support don't matter much."

Everything she's saying is true. I can feel it. The more she talks, the more understood I feel.

"Our parents are not very good at getting to the root of things," Gen continues. "Maybe that's just a generational thing, maybe it's because of their own family upbringings, I don't know. But you wanted the deeper stuff. And I get that because I was the same way – *am* the same way." She pauses. "And I think something about being with Ryan and his family fulfilled that for you. So you did anything to protect that and keep it close to you. Even if it meant pushing your own family away. As for the anxiety that you talk about in the letter…" She pauses again, shrugs and says, "It's so clear to me now that you've always had that. You were an anxious kid growing up. I think that's why you always liked painting so much because it was solitary and relaxing and you didn't have to worry about anything else. But then when our parents started turning your painting into this tool to get you places in life, it became an invasion of that sacred space for you. Which made you more anxious because you wanted to do things your own way but also didn't want to disappoint our parents." She throws her hands up as if exasperated.

"And by the time you got to college, painting had become this academic servitude where, if you didn't use it to get good grades or prove yourself as an artist, you were told that meant you weren't good enough. So I get it now. I can see why someone like Ryan was so attractive to you. He was a way out. He wanted to be in the art show more than you did. You were already falling out of love with your art. You sent me that birthday letter the summer before instead of a painting like you'd been doing since I was 12." Gen pauses again, playing with a piece of her hair. "And you knew you'd never be able to explain it to our parents. Because you'd never been able to explain *anything* emotional to them before. Or express yourself emotionally or get emotional advice about anything. Because they had more important things on their minds, like how much they wanted to fix their own unhappiness and have a successful family. And I know this because it was the same for me as well. It wouldn't have been exactly the same for Peter, though; they were still happy that early on. Peter was almost in college by the time our parents really started to go at each other. So he wouldn't have been around for the worst of it, not like you and me were. But especially you, during that last year of high school when they got divorced."

The words flow out of her freely and quickly, like she's piecing together this part about Peter as she goes. Everything falling into its place.

"Why do you think you're only just understanding this all now?" I ask.

She fiddles with a loose piece of thread on her shirt's hem. "I don't know. I've become wiser with age? I'm less self-centred now?"

"I wouldn't say you were self-centred," I reply.

"What would you say I was, then?"

I think carefully for a moment. "Young. Misguided."

She gives a half shrug. "Aren't we all, in the beginning? And even still, later in life." Gen lies down on the couch, her feet at one end, head on a pillow staring up at the ceiling. "I just realized something."

"What's that?"

"All this time, our parents have been thinking, if only you hadn't gone to school so far away, if only you hadn't met Ryan, if only Mom hadn't gone to the art show, none of this would have happened. And I've been thinking, if only I hadn't blabbed to Mom and Dad about you giving your art show spot to Ryan, if only I'd been a better sister, if only I'd said this or done that, none of this would have happened. But it's not true at all; it entirely misses the point. I think your falling-out with us still would have happened."

"Why do you say that?"

"Because of the nature of our family, of our parents. Because of your nature. Because of your naïvety, and mine. All that other stuff?" She waves a hand again. "It's just situational white noise. Circumstantial. I have a feeling that no matter what the context was, you eventually would have disowned us. Isn't that sad?"

I don't say anything immediately and instead ponder the thought. *Is* it sad? Or is it just a natural fact of family life? A family that can't figure out how to communicate with each other isn't uncommon. People who share parents and who have lived with each other from childhood to teen to adulthood – the only thing they have to prepare them in the world is their parents. But what if what their parents are teaching and passing on isn't right for them? "Right" isn't the correct word...I'm not sure what is. Adequate? All I know is that there's so much room for error when starting a family. Something is bound to go wrong.

"No, I don't think it's sad," I reply. "I think it's...beautiful."

Gen lifts her head to look at me and frowns. "Um, care to explain?"

I lean back in the armchair and hug my knees close, smiling ever so slightly. I feel so at peace all of a sudden. Well, more at peace than usual. "There's beauty in all of this. It's beautiful that your sister – me, I guess – evolved as a person so quickly, grew up so fast going through this falling out. She put a stop to this pattern in our family, this pattern where emotions get left to rot or burst. Where things get left unsaid, or they aren't said enough. Living Claire is...free to be her true self. To really be heard and seen. And maybe the cost of getting those things had to be her own family. She – I – intuitively knew that. And I can't imagine it would have been an easy thing to accept and act on. But I think there's beauty in her growth, even though it meant she grew apart from where she'd come from."

Gen flops her head back onto the pillow and is silent for a moment. Then she reaches up, rubbing her eyes. I can tell they've started to water. "I've never thought of it like that before." Her voice is thick. "And I'm not even mad about it, because yeah, you're right. You're totally right. She became herself."

I look down at the carpet and say carefully, "And maybe you *hadn't* yet, until this year. Or this week even."

Gen lets out a big sigh. "I can't even argue with that either," she says, giving a half laugh and pitiful shrug, "because it's true. My little sister evolved faster than I did. Who would have thought?" She sits up on the couch and grabs a tissue from the side table, blows her nose. "I just wish I could have been part of her evolution and not a reason for her to have evolved away from me."

"But you didn't know. You couldn't have known how to handle it. You didn't have the skills that you have now."

Gen scoffs. "Skills? What skills..."

"Well, talking to ghosts, for one," I say with a smirk. "But seriously, though. The skills you get as you grow as a person. Things like…" I get up and float over to the window, where the sun's light is barely peeking out from behind the building across the road. "Things like introspection, reflection, communication, emotional moderation."

"Wow," Gen says. "Those sound a bit too ethereal and deep for me."

I turn around. "That's just what I mean. You've never been good at any of those things. You were always such an outward person. I was very inward. I would think about things too much. You wouldn't think about things enough. You wouldn't process. I over-processed until I created my own realities of what I thought was the truth. You under-processed as a way to keep moving forward. I always admired you for that, actually. The ability to be present and forge ahead."

"Can't say we weren't a dynamic duo," Gen says, raising her brows. She sighs again. "You're right, though. Why are you more right as a ghost than your live self?"

I feign a look of disgust. "I was always right; you just never listened."

Gen laughs and throws up her hands. "Again, you're probably right."

Her words remind me of something that I still need to tell her. Something I still need to figure out. "Speaking of me being alive..." I glide across the room to the bookcase, pensive for a moment, then turn around. "It's not a matter of 'when I was alive'; I *am* still alive. I know that I am, and you know it too."

Gen nods slowly, her eyes locked on some point on the wall. "Right. I don't know how it's possible," she says, "but it's true. You are Schrödinger's cat."

I crinkle my nose. "I'm what?"

Gen looks at me. "You don't remember Schrödinger's cat theory? It's Philosophy 101."

I shake my head.

Gen leans forward on the couch. "If you put a cat and some poison together in a box, you can't know whether or not the cat is dead or alive until you open the box and find out. Thus, until you do, the cat is both dead *and* alive."

"Ohhh," I say, hovering back to the window, my hand on my chin, something clicking in my thoughts. "That *is* interesting." I'm prickling all over at what Gen's just told me. There's something to it, this cat philosophy. My soul knows it. My mind is racing, but I speak slowly. "So maybe you're saying...this timeline we're in is the box...I'm the cat...who's both dead *and* alive..."

"Technically, you're just the dead cat. Living Claire is the live one," Gen adds bluntly, then shrugs a "sorry" at me.

She's right, though. I'm only one half of the cat puzzle. I look out the window, down at the cars steadily moving by. "But what's the poison?" I frown, my mouth going taut as I think.

"And how on earth are we ever supposed to figure out what it is?" I hear Gen say.

Slowly, I turn around. "I think I'm going to get hit by a car."

She squints her eyes at me questioningly. "Okay, that was fast. How do you know that?"

I float over to the couch and sit next to Gen. "I don't know for sure, but I just have a feeling. Earlier today, when I was trying to get back here, a car drove through me, and I had this overwhelming sense of déjà vu."

Gen adjusts herself on the couch and says, "Can ghosts get déjà vu? How is that even possible?"

I shrug. "I don't know. All I know is that the car approached me, and I felt like I'd been there before, maybe not necessarily in that exact spot, but in that position, that circumstance. The vulnerability of being in front of an oncoming car. A dog barked, someone laughed. It was like this script played out that I'd already experienced before. And then I actually flinched when the car went through me. I even felt it drag me a bit as it threw me off balance."

Gen gives a little gasp. "Your body remembered something."

I shake my head. "No, not my body," I say. "My soul."

Gen holds out her arm. "I just got chills," she says, running a hand over her wrist. "What does this all mean?"

"I'm not sure," I reply. "I just know that I have to protect my soul. If I'm not dead yet, then there must be some way to stop my death from happening."

"Wait," Gen says, holding up a hand. "Are you saying that you're...from the future?"

It would make sense if I were, wouldn't it? The details don't really matter, though. The only thing that matters is stopping my death. Figuring out the poison that triggers the philosophy. The car must be the poison, right? But that's such a random thing. Accidents happen all the time; how can we ever track down the exact car, place and time where I might potentially get run over? Not to mention that that may not even be exactly how I die. Maybe I'm the one driving the car. I'm only going off of speculation and feeling at this point. That being said, my ghostly intuition hasn't been wrong yet.

Suddenly, a thought occurs to me.

"What if I die tomorrow before you get a chance to talk to me at the event?"

Gen's face freezes. I can see her mind working behind her eyes. "Oh my God," she says. "That makes sense...I have to *save* you! I knew there was this bigger reason behind why I felt I needed to see you tomorrow."

As she says those words, something in me crumples, drops. Something's not right. I feel so heavy again. "Wait," I say, "that's not it."

But the idea has gained momentum in my sister's head. She stands up from the couch and paces in front of the mantle. "Do you think I should try to find you tonight? What if you're in danger already? This is crazy. We need to do something."

The more Gen talks, the heavier I feel myself becoming in this realm. That's when I know with all my heart and soul that it's Gen; she's the poison. The more she wants to talk to me – living me – the more ghostly I can feel myself becoming. The more my death becomes an absolute. That's been the pattern the last few days. Her actions put my demise into motion somehow. Maybe now, or maybe later, but either way – the craving she has for our sisterhood bond to be restored is doomed. A destiny that can never happen. A fate worth avoiding.

Silently, I watch my sister pace back and forth; I just don't have the heart to tell her quite yet.

* * *

As Genevieve made herself some tea to try to calm her nerves, she remembered a particularly warm July day from their childhood. School had just ended the week before, and she and Claire had been wanting to go on a bike ride for what seemed like ages. Finally, they were free of school obligations, and their parents were happy enough to see them out of the house for a few hours, so both girls had packed a lunch complete with peanut butter saltine-cracker sandwiches, fruit rollups, juice boxes, rolled up pieces of ham, and celery with cheese. Claire grabbed her pack of tarot cards and the accompanying beginner's guide book while Genevieve packed a blanket and the dogs' leashes, mostly as a precaution.

They got on their bikes, and with Jezebel and Sparky loose at their sides, the two sisters had set off down the road. They knew exactly where they wanted to go, and their neighbours were no strangers to seeing the girls biking around with the dogs.

Genevieve led them down a dead-end dirt road where there was a beautiful property at the end with acres and acres of fields and pond. The girls often snuck along the side of the property to sit by the fence line under a big oak tree. Being the older dog, Jezebel liked to rest with the girls on the blanket, while Sparky roamed closely nearby, never straying far. The owner's house could be seen through the trees, but the girls had never once been caught, nor had they ever seen the owners.

Genevieve wasn't into tarot as much as Claire, but she had always enjoyed getting a reading done from her little sister and seeing what the different cards meant. She recalled that reading now, in light of what ghost Claire had just said.

On that day under the tree, Claire had dealt the Eight of Cups upright, the Wheel of Fortune in reverse, and the Four of Wands in reverse for Genevieve. Claire happily read from her tarot book the meanings of the cards, and Genevieve never forgot her saying that the Wheel of Fortune was telling her to break negative cycles and to change her destiny, but Genevieve thought that was silly because destiny was fixed, so how could she change it? Whatever was meant to be was always what was going to happen anyway – that's how she saw things. Claire told her she was wrong, though, and that every choice she made had a consequence, a different domino effect.

The girls argued about it for the rest of the picnic and then later asked their dad, who then told them about the butterfly effect. A chaos theory, he'd said. *Butterfly flaps its wings on one side of Earth, and a tornado happens on the other.* Claire had gleefully turned to her older sister and said, *See? Told ya!*

Genevieve was only thirteen years old at the time, and though she was the older sister, she still didn't quite get it. Now, though, she thought perhaps she might.

* * *

After Gen finally goes to sleep, I float around her apartment all night, trying to come up with an idea for how to avoid my death but still allow Gen to reunite with living Claire. After all of this time, she's finally ready to talk to her in a productive way. She understands on a whole new level why Claire left the family. She's forgiven her. She's not mad anymore. She's hopeful. And, miraculously, the opportunity to talk to her – me – has presented itself.

And yet, it's all wrong. I can't imagine why it has to be this way, but I'm living proof (ha) that something about their reunion is ill fated. No matter how much floating around I do, though, my mind is blank. I can't think of a single course of action that would save both of us.

How am I ever going to tell Gen? What will she do if I tell her? I don't want to crush her. Living me has already done that enough. When Gen makes up her mind about something, that's it. It's always been her way or the highway. She's never taken bad news well.

I'm reminded of the time when a bunch of her friends suddenly couldn't come to her eighth birthday party because of a fluke summer cold going around. Only two out of the ten kids could show up, but she wanted it to be all or nothing. Our parents wouldn't hear of it, though, so her party went ahead with just me, Gen, and two of her friends. She was mopey the whole time.

Finally, the sun rises, and it's not long before Gen bounds out of bed.

"Oh my God, I'm so nervous!" she says as she runs around getting ready.

While she showers, I play with a stress ball that Gen has at her desk, rolling it across the surface between my hands. I squeeze the ball, the yellow foam puffing between my fingers. My skin is still quite see-through, but my physical grasp on things has become so much stronger. I don't even have to try. This must be what happens to ghosts who have unfinished business, as they say. I think it's the living that keep us from moving on. Someone wishes they'd said this or that, wishes they'd been there, done something differently. Their grief and regret keep us alive as these physical manifestations because that's what they long for: our earthly, animated selves back on Earth. But souls aren't meant to be ghosts forever. I don't want to be stuck here like this indefinitely.

I start to think about what will happen to me if I do tell Gen, and she decides not to talk to living Claire. Will I cease to exist? Will it hurt? Will I be stuck in some other limbo? Or will I still remain here? I can only take comfort in the fact that living me still exists, and she's all that matters; I'm just a ghost. A double-image of her.

I can feel the anxiety bubbling up in me. The more concrete my presence has become, the more human I've been feeling. More emotions, more racing thoughts. That low-key bliss isn't lasting. That endless positivity is disappearing. I'm starting to feel more like myself, which would normally be a good thing. But I don't think it is, in this case. I feel so heavy.

I was never good at delivering bad news to Gen. In fact, I actively avoided it most of our childhood, or I would get Peter to do it. Or I just wouldn't say anything at all, disappearing into myself, slipping away from reality into my paintings. And then later, Gen would get so mad at me for not telling her. Like that time I "forgot" to tell her I lost her mermaid necklace in the sand at the beach, and she spent all afternoon looking for it in the car. Gen always had a bit of a temper, but in this case, I'm not worried about her being mad; I'm worried about breaking her heart.

Maybe it's possible that I'm wrong about all of this. I wish I had a sure way of knowing. I wish I could distinctly remember something – anything – about my death. And not just déjà vu. I mean an actual memory of the events and days leading up to it. There isn't enough time to figure that out.

Gen comes out of the shower and finishes getting dressed.

"How do I look?" she asks. "Do I look like I have my shit together?"

She's wearing slim black pants, ankle books, an oversized moss-green sweater and a grey knit circle scarf. Her ashy blond hair has been dried roughly with the blow dryer but somehow still looks styled. She must have put some product in it.

I smile weakly. "Sure, looks great."

Gen heads into the kitchen. "I know I've still got a while before I see living Claire, but I want to get there early to make sure I'm in the right place," she says, putting some bread in the toaster. "But also, if I'm meant to save her – you, then I should really be there as early as possible." She pauses. "I'm actually so excited to see her. I feel this will be a fresh start for both of us."

"What if she doesn't feel the same?" I ask.

Gen turns around, her smile fading. "I hadn't really thought about that. I just figured it would go well...I think you being here is kind of giving me your blessing, isn't it?"

My innards tumble, and I look at the ground. I feel like I might throw up.

"Gen," I say. "I need to tell you something."

* * *

While she listened to her ghostly sister, Genevieve buttered and jammed her toast. As she chewed slowly, she felt the certainty drain from her, replaced by a sickening doubt. Just like that, she wasn't so sure about going to see Claire. Ghost Claire seemed to think that it would be Genevieve's reunion with Claire that sent Claire to her death. Genevieve didn't see how the two were related or how it was possible. Denial replaced her doubt. Ghost Claire had to be wrong. How was it possible for someone to die simply because someone else talked to them?

Genevieve was reminded once again of the butterfly effect. Other philosophies came into her mind too – Occam's Razor, Murphy's Law. Was it true? Were she and her sister doomed to be separated forever? Genevieve didn't want to believe it.

She asked the ghost for proof, something to sell the idea to her. Genevieve just couldn't accept that she was the deadly substance.

In response, ghost Claire went over to Gen's desk, picked up the stack of sticky notes and tossed it across the room, where it landed on the carpeted floor with a thud. *Bit dramatic,* Genevieve thought. But she got the point. Her sister's ghost was evolving, it seemed, becoming stronger, tethered to Earth – but was it really because of Genevieve's intention to see Claire? Was she to blame?

Genevieve decided that she couldn't not go at all. She had to at least be at the location and think things through. Then she would decide.

The art fair was only a short subway ride and a walk away. Genevieve could barely focus on the crowds around her as she sat on the train, then walked out and up to street level. Her sister's ghost shadowed her the entire way. Genevieve knew Ghost Claire wasn't happy about this, but after all this build-up, Genevieve couldn't give up that easily. She was a mixed bag of emotions. She felt as if she were tempting fate, taunting death, by going to the fair. None of it seemed real, but she had to keep reminding herself that it was.

The art fair always took place in the old Victorian atrium downtown. A long time ago, it used to be an indoor swimming pool, so there was a large sunken portion in the middle, with a walkway all around, and an upper balcony that wrapped around up top. The atrium was echoey, open and airy with glass windows everywhere and green iron framework. It was a stunning building both inside and out, and as Genevieve approached it, she felt a rush of emotions swell up inside. She and Claire used to come here every year for the art fair. It had been several years at least since they'd attended together. But somewhere in that glass cage was her sister, the living one.

* * *

Gen is enthralled by the atrium up ahead. I watch her move towards it like a magnet.

Since this morning, the sun has gone away, replaced by an overcast sky. It looks like it might rain, but I imagine that the air has become too chilly for that.

My body is still partially transparent but feels like lead. It's an effort to keep up with Gen's fast pace. For just once, I wish she would listen to me. As kids, she never listened or trusted that I might know something she didn't. Peter acted the same way to me too. Even our parents constantly gave me the impression that they didn't believe I knew what I was doing most of the time, that I couldn't possibly know what was best for me or how to look after myself. Was it because I was the youngest? Or was it more of an attack on my withdrawn personality? It doesn't matter now. But of all the times I've wished Gen would just trust me, this is the most important one.

"Gen," I say as she weaves her way through a throng of people waiting to cross the road. "Gen! Listen to me."

My sister barely glances back. "I know what you're going to say," she says. "I just need to see for myself."

She's playing with my life – Claire's life. All for the sake of satisfying her own desire to reunite with her sister. What if living Claire doesn't want to? Then this will all have been for nothing, and I may still die somehow.

"Gen, please stop," I say and instinctively grab her arm. My hand drags through it, and she turns abruptly. Looks down at her arm.

"I felt that," she says.

We've paused just outside the atrium doors.

"You're killing me," I say desperately. "Don't you see that?"

Finally, Gen looks at me. I see her mind working. Then she looks around at the people walking into the art fair, the bus passing by, a father leading his son by the hand. She rubs her eyes for a moment.

"Claire," she says, "I just want to see her. Just for a moment. How can that be so bad?"

"You're looking at her *right now*," I plead. "And I'm telling you. This is wrong. Can't you just respect my wishes? I don't want to be stuck here forever." For the first time in three days, I feel true terror at such a thought.

My sister swallows, says nothing for a few moments. Her hands are shaking. "How about this: I promise I won't talk to her. I just want to look."

And with that, she turns into the atrium.

* * *

The atrium had a faint buzz about it. Low murmurs echoed throughout. There were multitudes of art booths and mini exhibitions set up all around on both levels. Painters, sketch artists, mixed-media pieces, sculptures, pottery, textiles and weavers, authors, poets, printmakers, zine booths, guitarists. There was even a small platform set up for a handful of modern dancers giving a beautiful performance.

The sunken pool area was straight ahead. Genevieve walked down into it and scanned people as she passed by. Her heart was pounding, and she couldn't stop shaking every few seconds. She walked by a booth selling tea, coffee and treats. The smells were heavenly.

In a sense, Genevieve almost hoped she *wouldn't* see Claire now, given all that had happened the last 24 hours, but she could say she at least tried. Everything felt so conflicting; she couldn't stop driving herself forward to wherever Claire was, but at the same time she doubted every step she took.

She had not seen her own sister, her first best friend, in over five years. More than anything, she wanted things to go back to the way they'd been. She just wanted Claire back in her life. She wanted her best friend back. Why did Claire have to hate her so much? Genevieve finally understood why Claire had to leave the family, but why did she have to leave Genevieve? She could never imagine herself doing the same to Claire, no matter how bad things ever got between them.

Perhaps that's what she really wanted to know. *Why me? Why leave me?*

She couldn't see Claire or Ryan anywhere. She decided to head up to the balcony to get a better view. Ghost Claire followed right behind.

Genevieve walked around the entire upper balcony in one full circuit without any luck before coming to the edge of the railing and scanning the crowd below again. Maybe Claire and Ryan had already been and gone. Maybe she'd missed them. Or maybe the meeting was just never meant to be.

Genevieve placed her hands on the railing and leant over slightly to see better, but Claire was nowhere. Her heart felt like it might break open her chest. Her stomach kept dropping. She never imagined she'd be this nervous to see Claire again. Perhaps it was the anticipation of being rejected by her sister once more, but in person rather than through email. Genevieve didn't know if she'd be able to handle that, and she realized how much she hated feeling unwanted. Even growing up,

Genevieve had always felt she needed Claire more than Claire needed her – always needing Claire to play with her, to listen, needing Claire to follow, to need Genevieve back.

The truth was, Genevieve didn't feel needed anywhere in life. Not by the daycare, not by her friends, not by her parents. Everyone was off living their own little lives, while she felt like she didn't have one. A ghost in her own life, drifting nowhere and largely unseen. Unknown.

This was normally something she would have confessed to Claire by now, during a late-night call on FaceTime, both of them with a cup of tea in hand. And Claire would have lent an ear, delivered her sage sisterly advice, that unconditional best-friend feedback. It was something they'd done for each other up until the end. Why did Claire not want that? Had she replaced Genevieve with a close circle of girlfriends? Or maybe it was Ryan whom Claire confided in regularly. The thought sent a pang through Genevieve's chest. She could only surmise that Claire had a life of some sort, and she'd been living it just fine without Genevieve for the past five years.

Genevieve turned to look at ghost Claire, who'd been standing next to her the whole time, looking out over the crowd. She still wore the boyfriend jeans and unbuttoned plaid shirt, sleeves rolled up, black tank tucked in. Her long, dark hair framed her delicate features. Ghost Claire looked just like she did when they were in their teens, except now her eyes haunted Genevieve pleadingly. Genevieve wanted more than ever to hug her. To tell her she was sorry. So incredibly sorry for not being the sister Claire had wanted. Everything she'd realized about herself, their family and their relationship had all come too late. Genevieve realized in that moment that that's what was clouding her judgement: the overwhelming desire to tell Claire, *I get it now. You can trust me again.* The deep craving for redemption and to prove to her living sister that she was ready to truly be there for her now. Genevieve had to know she'd at least tried to get this message to Claire, and then Claire could decide for herself at that point. They could start over.

Start over…Genevieve realized how ridiculous that sounded.

Start.

Over.

Start…where?

Starting over implied acting like nothing had happened. Images flashed through her mind of coming face to face with Claire, stumbling for words. What could really be said in that moment other than, "I'm sorry"? It wouldn't be enough. She wanted it to be, but that was something Genevieve could never control. That's what she wanted – she wanted the control back, just like she always did. Was it worth the risk, though?

Genevieve finally understood ghost Claire.

She turned away from the silent ghost and back to the crowd; that's when she saw her. Genevieve's breath caught in her throat, and her heart met her gut.

Claire was at the concession stand with Ryan, just below Genevieve, right where she had walked earlier. Her dark brown hair had some highlights in it and was a fair bit shorter now. She wore a similar style of outfit to Genevieve: black leggings, an oversized sweater, maroon coat, brown ankle boots, and a cream-coloured circle scarf. But it was her – the round face, the long painter's fingers.

Ryan stood next to her, arm wrapped around her waist while they waited for their drinks. Claire was smiling as she took in the surroundings. Ryan said something that made her laugh. They looked happy.

Genevieve was mesmerized. She watched Claire take the tea she'd ordered and set it down on the side table, where she removed the lid, added some milk and sugar, then gave it a stir. Just like they both used to drink it together. Some things never change. And perhaps they never would.

Then, just like that, with their drinks in hand, Ryan and Claire continued walking in Genevieve's direction, admiring the artwork, until they disappeared under the balcony beneath her. Genevieve let out a few gulps of breath. She knew she would not follow them. She could not bring herself to jeopardize her sister's life. If they weren't meant to be family, who was she to try to change that?

Genevieve's chest welled until the emotion silently surged out of her breath, leaked from her eyes. She felt like she was expelling something as she cried at the balcony. The mistakes of her family, her lack of awareness as a sister, the emptiness she'd been feeling lately in life. Though she'd cried a handful of times the past few days, this time felt different. More final. Like it was the last cry she was going to need for a while.

Something cold enveloped her and she shivered. Remembering ghost Claire, Genevieve turned around, but the ghost was gone. Only a crowd of strangers passed by.

Through the glass outside, it had begun to snow.

* * *

I stand next to Gen, staring into her soul one final time. Then she looks back down at the crowd, and I know she's seen them. Her gaze is transfixed, and I drift backwards a few steps, watch her from behind. My sister at the balcony. What will she do? I'm tempted to run and hide, a reflex from when I was a kid.

I worry that I haven't done enough, said enough, to prevent my demise. It's why I'm here. Finally, I can really be here for my sister in ways that she doesn't understand yet; it's something I didn't excel at growing up. She wasn't perfect, but neither was I. Still, I worry it's not enough. She's always been so strong willed, so insecurely stuck in her own ways.

I watch my sister at the balcony, my life in her hands. She can't always have what she wants, but she can always get what she needs. I hope she knows that. There are other ways for her to move on from this.

I send out all my trust to her, and slowly I begin to feel lighter. Gen is making the choice. I can feel it. She's deciding. She's setting me free.

The heaviness dissipates; I feel like I may float away at any moment I'm so light. The low-key bliss pours into the top of my crown like water rushing into a dry channel after a rainfall. If I could cry, I would. I know that Gen is; I can see her shoulders moving. She's letting me go. All I feel is love for her. Unconditional love and trust.

I look down at my hands; they're so translucent, fading right before my eyes. I smile and look up at Gen. She's still leaning on the balcony, crying. I can no longer find my voice, so I glide towards her, smiling still, my arms outstretched in the hug that she'll never really feel.

I envelop my sister, closing my eyes and resting my head on her back. But I've become so light, as light as the air at the top of the atmosphere, that I simply move through her, my heart passing through hers, the last thing I feel.

11 days later

The airport was no more crowded than usual, or at least that's what Genevieve guessed. It had been a while since she'd been in one. She sat in the lounge of gate C21 with her carry-on resting on the floor, and a backpack on the seat next to her. This was her moment, she realized. This calm between the life she was leaving behind, and the decision she was about to make manifest.

Her parents had not been happy she'd up and quit her job at the daycare and broken her one-year lease. She hadn't cared, though; she'd paid the fine for the lease break and ignored all the confused, judgmental looks she'd been given at the daycare. They asked what she was going to do, and did she have another job lined up? When she'd told them no, she was going away somewhere and had no plans, she'd simply received blank stares. It was the most freeing feeling.

On the weekend, Genevieve delivered some of her personal belongings to her dad's house and gave some furniture to Peter and his girlfriend. The rest she'd sold or donated. Her wardrobe had been purged. She'd stuffed her checked luggage with essentials, including a brand-new journal she'd purchased for the trip, and had put her laptop and valuables in her carry-on. She had enough saved up in the bank that she could do this for a short while. She felt lighter than ever.

Genevieve kept replaying the moment in the atrium when she'd seen her sister, her real, living sister, Claire. The more she thought about it, the more it felt like a dream. Had it really happened? Of course it had, but she had no one to share it with. Maybe that's why it felt so dreamlike. And maybe it would be that way forever, internalized, only hers to look at when she needed. She was actually glad she got to see Ryan there, too. The way he'd tenderly wrapped his arm around Claire while they waited for their drinks, the way he'd so easily made her laugh, how his hand enveloped hers as they'd walked – Genevieve now felt that whatever part he had or hadn't played in Claire's fallout with her family, there was no denying they were a couple truly in love with each other. Genevieve hadn't really got to witness that on the spring break trip, and perhaps that had fuelled her doubts about Ryan, but she let all that go now. She trusted Claire.

As for ghost Claire, Genevieve wished she could have gotten a chance to say goodbye, but it all happened so fast, and she knew it couldn't have been any other way. And at the same time, she also knew that wherever ghost Claire was, she understood.

Genevieve thought about the trip ahead. Was she

crazy for buying a one-way ticket? Probably. But it felt right. It felt exhilarating. For the first time in possibly her whole life, Genevieve felt truly alive. She understood now that she had not been living those past five years; she'd been waiting. Waiting for the naïvety of her childhood to kick in and save her, make everything right again, while everyone else moved on. Her parents had made mistakes, but they were only human. They were on their own journey. Even Claire had made mistakes in the way she'd handled things. But she was also on her own journey...just not together with Genevieve.

She had to trust that someday, she would see her sister again. But if that was to be the case, she knew she must let Claire come to her when she was ready. If she ever was.

For the past week, Genevieve had been debating whether or not to tell her parents about the newfound understanding she'd gleaned from reading those emails again, and the insights from ghost Claire. Would it matter now? Would they even understand? For the time being, she decided to keep it to herself. It would just be one of the many things she'd be figuring out what to do with on this trip.

The flight attendant opened up the boarding call to all remaining passengers for flight KA577 to Bali. That was Genevieve. She put on her backpack, grabbed her carry-on and joined the lineup. Peope shuffled forward slowly, showing their tickets and passports to the attendant.

Genevieve's stomach buzzed as she tugged her carry-on down the loading bridge, the hum of the plane's enginge just around the bend. It was a trip she'd always thought she'd be making with her sister and she felt a pang in her heart, not having Claire's beaming face next to her. But Genevieve knew she was ready to do it alone. Ready to make better choices. To be happier. To let go.

Anything could happen.

EMMA KVĚTNA

Acknowledgments

This book began as a project for NaNoWriMo in 2022 when I started meeting weekly with my local writers' group. The support it received along the way was integral to me completing the drafts and reaching publication. Thank you to all the members of my writers' group, Paper Mates, for their encouragement and advice whenever I shared snippets of the work-in-progress. Thank you to my beta readers James, Camilla, Jillian, Lisa, Allison, Thekla, Lauren, and Barbara, for taking the time to provide invaluable feedback. Thank you to Carissa for letting me stay at her farm while I made final revisions on the book. Thank you to my editor, Chelsea Comeau, for her brilliant and insightful copyediting. Thank you to Mom and Dad, and all my other friends and family who helped support me with this book – you know who you are. And thank you to my sister; I will always love you.

EMMA KVĚTNA

About the Author

Emma Května is a Canadian writer and poet currently based in Nova Scotia on the unceded territory of the Mi'kmaq people. Her writing has appeared in *Filling Station, Planisphere Quarterly, Bell Press* and *FAYD Digital.* She is also a songwriter, performer, artist, and host of the podcast *The Art of Existing.* Learn more about her writing classes and other offers online at <u>emmakvetna.com</u>.